BEYOND
THE GATES
OF
HERCULES

By Elizabeth Borton de Treviño

Nacar, the White Deer

I, Juan de Pareja

Casilda of the Rising Moon

Turi's Poppa

Here Is Mexico

Beyond the Gates of Hercules

BEYOND THE GATES OF HERCULES

A TALE OF
THE LOST ATLANTIS

by Elizabeth Borton
de Treviño

An Ariel Book

Farrar, Straus & Giroux

New York

To Jeane Campbell Chapman

FOREWORD

IT was my father who first interested me in the Lost
Atlantis. As a child I spent every summer at the
seashore, and my imagination was always engaged by the
mystery of the sea, the wonders it enclosed. All my life,
I have been fascinated by imaginative speculation, and
in my maturity I have come to believe that legends and
folk memory come as near the truth, in many instances,
as material proofs of life in the past, such as pottery
shards, rocks, or artifacts. It has interested me that repu-
table scholars in recent years have advanced the theory
that when legends of different peoples coincide, one
should assume that, encapsuled in poetry and imagery,
history has been preserved. Some scholars suggest that
even the hierarchies of the Gods—Greek, Celtic, Egyp-

tian, American, all the others—were not invented by literary geniuses of the past but were simply folk biography, the gods having been living heroes who were deified after death and immortalized in legends that really recounted their exploits, exaggerated and endowed with magic as each storyteller added details to the remembered outline.

Looked at in this way, the persistent legend of the Lost Continent, which went down into the sea in several harrowing convulsions, becomes as real as the story of the Ark, which indeed was true, since that strange craft has been found, preserved in ice, on the slopes of Mt. Ararat.

I offer my tale of the Lost Atlantis, therefore, with the hope that it will be read as something that truly "might have been"—the story of a past in which once in a while we may see prophecies of what was to come: a tale which may, fleetingly, awaken a strange feeling of nostalgia.

Elizabeth Borton de Treviño

BEYOND
THE GATES
OF
HERCULES

PROLOGUE

THE birthing room, as was the custom, had been built away from the dwelling, and as near the sea as possible, so that the steady rhythm of the waves could calm and help the mother in her labor. Mara was puzzled, and a little frightened, at the time she had spent trying to bring this child into the world. Previously, she had given her husband four sturdy sons, and with a minimum of effort. But now the sun had risen and sunk into the sea twice, and still she struggled. She felt her strength fast ebbing, and she feared she might slip away with the retreating tide, and the little unborn child with her.

She called her serving maid. It was early on the third morning.

"Help me up," she whispered.

"But, my lady . . ."

"I must look out to sea. I want to make a promise."

The sea was heaving but quiet, silver, just beginning to take on the rosy tints of dawn.

"Great Ocean, I promise him to you! He shall be your priest! Only help me! Bring him to light!"

Not much later, twin girls were born.

They were as alike as two drops of water, as the two bars of sunlight that pierced through the narrow openings of the room to the east.

One she called Atlanta and promised as a priestess. The other was given the name of Aurora for the dawn, which had burst into glory over the sea and the land as the babes came into the world. They were small and perfect, and both opened their eyes to stare at their mother.

She sent the maid for her husband, Drako, who came hurrying through the fresh cool air of morning. He pressed his wife's hair back from her brow with a tender hand, and said, "I thank you for these two young lives. They are beautiful."

After he had seen and praised the twin baby girls, he sent for a feather and blue paint. When these were brought, he drew a small circle in blue on the forehead of one. "This shall be Atlanta," he said. "Now we shall know them apart."

I

1

THE family was called "Those who live by the
Arches," for their home was near the place where
strange rock formations had been bitten and carved by
wind and water until they formed a long series of arches,
through which the water rushed with a roar at high tide.
At low tide the children played on the white and gold
sand beaches under the arches. They had discovered and
explored many of the caves that hid back of the arches,
which contained treasures that the children imagined
were of great value—shells and smooth pieces of driftwood, and colored stones. Beyond were several mysterious
caves where strange lights could be glimpsed within.

The Archers, as they were often called, lived simply
with many helpers; they cultivated vast fields of the

flowering iris which yielded saffron—the spicy, deep-golden pistil of the flower. This was gathered from the blooms, packed into cakes which were dried carefully above ovens, and sold to the Egyptian traders who sailed in their light boats across the seas to load the fragrant cakes into their holds. Saffron was much treasured to color royal garments and to flavor the foods of the rich, in Egypt and in other countries within the Gates of Hercules. The Archers kept bees too, and sold the honey, and pressed the wax into candles which they perfumed with flower oils for lighting the temples. The people themselves used few candles or lamps, for they were a hard-working and simple race who lived by the light of the sun and the moon and suited their activities to whatever light the heavens supplied.

Their home was on the island-continent of Poseida, part of the great kingdom called Atlantis. Poseida looked toward Egypt. Another island, peopled by Atlanteans of another race—small, dark, hairy men—stretched out toward the cold, snowy, mysterious lands of the north. There were other islands too, but all owed sovereignty to the central continent of Atlantis. The Council of Rulers there were chosen for their wisdom and justice, and all the islands were bound to live by a code which honored work and sharing, praised intellectual eminence, taught courtesy and kindliness, and outlawed pride, thievery, and deceit.

Mara's father was a magistrate in the nearby port of Hesperidia, and the four brothers of Aurora and Atlanta were often there when they were small, studying under his grandfatherly eye.

The youngest boy, Baka, who was brilliant, had been taken in as an apprentice by the great astronomer-physicist, Lakon, in his studio in the science laboratory on a hilltop overlooking the port. Baka was not tall and handsome like his brothers; he seemed to be a throwback to some forgotten ancestor of another island, for he was short and unattractive and his hair was straight and lank. His keen eyes were set deep into the sockets and gave him a suspicious expression. Lakon praised him and told the boys' parents that Baka would be a great name some day, for he had a natural gift for mathematics and enormous powers of concentration.

There were three older brothers. Aram, the eldest, was a student mariner at the naval training school in Hesperidia. He was learning the lore and the arts of the sea. In a few years more he would be a shipbuilder and a captain, and would carry the products of Poseida to all the known world. The family was happy when Aram's white-sailed small skiff came into the home cove, for he was always kind and cheerful.

Ramo and Akil remained at home to help their father with the duties of the saffron fields and the administration of the family business.

The three older boys were dark, like their father and Baka, but unlike Baka, they were tall and strong. Akil especially had the strength and agility of an antlered deer, but in character he was gentle and quiet-spoken.

Baka was the only one of the family who lacked the quality many of the Poseidans had . . . the ability to communicate without words, by means of thought alone. Atlanta could read and send thoughts with ease, and Aurora had much of the same gift. Aram and Akil could receive thoughts, which came to them in the form of sudden visions, just as Drako, their father, could. Ramo, like his sisters and his mother, was very sensitive, and could go for days without speaking, enjoying all the thoughts that came his way, and sending out his own.

Baka envied his brothers and sisters this power. It made him feel left out and lost, and also it made him angry and resentful. Usually he pretended not to care, and he sometimes said this was just foolish old magic, and that it had nothing to do with the modern scientific world.

While the brothers were dark, olive-skinned, with black hair, the two girls were golden like their mother. They played on the beaches, in the sunshine, and their skin had darkened like warm honey. Their hair was thick, the color of saffron, and they had eyes like the Great Ocean—gray and green and blue, changing at every hour of the day.

Aurora and Atlanta were inseparable, and when they were small they delighted in being the mirror images of each other. Atlanta sometimes scrubbed away her blue mark and painted it on Aurora's brow, but this joke palled after a time, and when they entered their teens, Atlanta often used a blue fillet to hold back her hair, while Aurora preferred a band of white. The girls began to accept that they were not in fact one person, as they had thought when they were small, but two, with different duties, who would lead dissimilar lives. Sometimes this troubled them.

On the day they celebrated their fourteenth birthday, they went in the early morning, as was the tradition in Poseida, to the cottage where they had been born: the birthing room, used now only by women who worked in the saffron fields and some of the women who helped weave and cook and spin in the Archer dwellings. The cottage was of stone, with windows to the east; it had the sparest of furnishings. On four stone legs stood the framework of a cot, made of light wood, with lacings of strong woven cord. To one side there was a stone stove on which was heated the sea water used to wash the mother and the babe.

Aurora stretched herself out upon the cot; Atlanta sat at the foot.

"Atlanta, what if one day we will lie here, waiting for the Great Ocean to help us bring a new life into being?"

"You may, Aurora. Not I. You know that I am promised to the priestesses who serve the sea gods. On this very day next year we will be parted, for then I must go to join them, to learn my duties."

Her voice was a tone or two lower than her sister's, and it was sad.

Aurora, who usually knew what Atlanta was thinking, said quickly, "Do not be unhappy. I will ask Father and Mother to let me go with you!"

But Atlanta shook her head. "They wish you to stay at their side. I know," she said. From infancy she had been able to read thoughts, and she was more adept at this than Aurora. "I am unhappy only at the thought of our parting," explained Atlanta, "not at the life I will live. I love the sea, our Great Ocean, the very water of Life! The Eternal Power! I will be proud to serve the sea gods to the very end."

Aurora trembled with fear, for she knew that the priestesses who served the sea sometimes sacrificed themselves to appease its anger. Only last year, after a terrible storm in which it seemed the Great Ocean would never stop raging, thrashing, and roaring, one of the priestesses had adorned herself in silks and jewels and had waded out into the deep, to give herself to the waters —after which they had calmed and subsided. It had been a solemn and beautiful ritual, like a wedding—but the young priestess was never seen again.

Atlanta fell into one of her trances, when she seemed to be looking into an endless future, when she appeared to be transfixed by Time into an eternal moment, motionless. Aurora felt a premonitory chill, for Atlanta often told the future after one of these seizures.

There was a silence. Nothing was heard but the soft steady breathing of the sea.

Then Atlanta moved and smiled. She touched her twin lovingly. "Our joy will come from the sea, yours and mine," she said confidently. "And always we will be joined in thought. Always."

2

THE saffron fields worked by the Archers and their helpers stretched along the coast for many miles, and the pungent scent was always in the air, in the rooms of their home, in their clothes.

Mara, who oversaw the drying and packing of the pistils, came to call her daughters.

As she appeared in the doorway of the hut, it seemed to the girls that their mother's gown, a simple robe held in at the waist by a woven cord, seemed to give off golden light.

"Mother!" Atlanta and Aurora ran to take her hand and touch it in reverence to their brows.

"My treasures, come. It is time to begin harvesting the pistils of the saffron, and I want you to follow after me into the fields. You must learn every step of our work with this sacred plant."

"Atlanta won't need to," offered Aurora. "I will do her part. She is going as a priestess in the next year."

"But meanwhile," put in her mother gently, "she should learn. It is always wise to learn new things and to understand the ways of the working world."

They went back, along a path on the cliffside beside the sounding sea, to their home. The dwelling was long, consisting of many rooms opening into one another, all facing the sea but flanked by broad shaded verandas on the land side.

"Put these on," said Mara, handing each girl a voluminous apron with large pockets in front and a broad-brimmed woven hat, to be tied on under the chin. "And tie these scarves over your noses. The scent is very strong there among the flowers, and at first it may make you dizzy."

The girls were excited, for the sacred fields were well patrolled and cared for by Drako's men, and they had never been allowed to set foot inside them before.

Following their mother, they saw that there were very narrow paths between the lines of planting, but they could walk on them only if they set one foot before the other and kept their balance. At first the girls were glad of the scarves tied over the lower part of their faces, for the fragrance was overpowering. Soon, however, their noses became immune to it, though their eyes stung and tears fell from them.

The plants were small, and so were the lily-like flowers, rearing up on stiff stalks from the leaves. They were pale blue and violet, with the deep golden pistil inside, the part of the flower for which the whole plant was cultivated.

Mara, standing among the plants, told her daughters, "This has been a sacred living thing for all the centuries of man's remembrance. Only our island can produce the lily which yields saffron. Centuries ago an angel came down from the sky regions and brought us the first bulbs; it was a being as radiant as light, who blinded the eyes of those who stared at him when he appeared. It was as if the sun were all around him, making him transparent and protecting him from our human eyes. He gave the three golden bulbs into the hands of one of your father's ancestors—a priestess, such as you will be, Atlanta!—and told her how to plant them, and he spoke to her, though only she could hear and understand his words.

" 'These are the Golden Apples of Hesperides,' he told her. 'Plant them, and tend them, and when the blossoms come, extract the golden spear at the heart of each flower. This little spear will provide you with fragrance, perfume for ointments, for the altars, and for the priestesses, with color for their sacred garments, and with flavor for the breads and cakes to be eaten on the great feast days.' "

Mara went on to tell her daughters that the angel had warned the priestess never to allow the bulbs to be taken off the island, for if they were carried away, there would be great trouble and suffering, the tides would rise and crush out homes and wash away the people, the sky would darken, and heaven would send down fire.

Aurora shivered at the vision her mother had called up.

"And did no one ever try—to steal them, Mother?"

"Strangers have tried. And once there was a sailor in a long boat who came secretly in the night, and beached his craft, and took away some of the bulbs. You know that the pressed pistils are sold all over the world, even across on the other side, and great quantities go to Egypt after every harvesting. But when the bulbs had been taken it happened as the angel had told. There were thunderings in the earth, and the sea rose and was angry and roared, and mountains opened their mouths and poured out fire. That is when Poseida was separated from the island to the north; in ancient times, our two islands were one."

The girls were silent and engrossed, listening.

"So it is not the pistil, the valuable part, that must stay here, but only the bulb, the seed of the plant," murmured Aurora.

"That is so. Now, take the blossoms softly, carefully, the whole blossom, but do not injure the stalk. That is the way. Come now, follow me, and gather the flowers, until the pockets in your aprons are filled."

The girls did as they were told, working in silence behind their mother. Bees buzzed among the flowers, but they did not sting, and the twins were not afraid of them.

When their aprons were full to overflowing with the

flowers, Mara led the girls to the drying sheds, which were constructed in a long series beyond the fields and toward the low-lying hills which marked the horizon. It was a fairly long walk in the bright sunshine, and the girls were beginning to feel weary when they came to where ovens were being heated for the drying of the pistils.

"First we will go to the plucking rooms," said Mara. The rooms were open on all sides, covered over, for shade, but latticed on the sea side, so as to temper the sea winds. Here six women, wearing silken nose scarves and saffron-stained coveralls, were working. They bowed to Mara, and went about their tasks, carefully taking the pistils from the blooms. The flowers themselves they cast into a great drum, where they would be allowed to disintegrate; the planters later would work them into the soil again, to enrich it for the next harvest.

"Now to the baking ovens."

Here the pistils, pressed by hand into almost solid blocks, were thoroughly dried on metal pans over ovens that were kept at a constant temperature. This was very skillful work, presided over by men who also prepared the earth and set out new crops of saffron from the carefully guarded bulbs of the plants.

The lesson over for the day, Mara led her daughters back to their home, where they were told to sit and meditate about the sacred flower and its properties.

When questions were allowed, Aurora asked, "And what of the angel who first brought the plant, Mother? Has anyone ever seen him again?"

"I cannot say," answered Mara, smiling at her daughter. "I will answer with another question. Suppose the angel would appear to you, would you tell of it?"

"I suppose not," stammered Aurora. "Not without asking his permission."

"He would not give permission," put in Atlanta quietly, and something in her manner settled the discussion. A fleeting thought darted through Aurora's mind. Perhaps Atlanta had seen him, the angel?

Mara was a tall woman, in the maturity of her strength and beauty. She had broad shoulders, strong feet and hands, and her skin had turned golden from the sun, like that of her twin daughters. Her eyes were very large, of a golden brown, under dark brows, and her heavy mane of light brown hair was held in place by bands of blue ribbon and tied at the nape of the neck with a wider band. Her dress was that of all the women, young and old, of Poseida—a washable thin stuff, gathered into folds at the shoulder, falling only to the knee, and held in at the waist by a woven girdle. She was bare-legged and wore sandals made of a sturdy sole, tied on with fiber thongs. Hanging by cords down her back was a broad-brimmed hat she could wear if the sun were directly overhead, or if it rained. Mara's dress was a faded violet in color; Atlanta's was sky blue, and Aurora's a pale green.

"You have much to learn, my daughters," Mara told them. "But quiet meditation will bring many things into your minds. The thoughts and plans and the wisdom of all time are all around us, if we can but make ourselves properly receptive."

Aurora asked, "Mother—and how can we know when

we receive wisdom? Were there not wicked, wrong thoughts, too, in the past? And couldn't they creep into our minds when we are waiting?"

Mara laid her strong hand on Aurora's breast. "We have a defense against the wrong thoughts, dear child. It is here. If you suppose you are thinking something that might not lead to good, lay your hand on your heart and ask would this thing I am thinking hurt anyone, destroy any beauty that I know, deprive any creature of its life and its place? Your heart will know. Your heart will tell you truly."

She went to the open doorway that gave onto the wide verandas surrounding the house.

"Stay here and meditate," she ordered. "I will go to meet your father and brothers, who are coming to us for the midday meal."

The two girls sat on low benches, legs crossed and feet turned under, hands softly folded.

As Atlanta meditated, she saw the sea rise before her inner eye, magnificent in beauty, flashing all the colors of the sky and the rainbow, plus its own emerald and jade. She felt her mind drawn into a deep cool peace, and a profound happiness stole through her senses.

Aurora saw the sea also, but suddenly upon that sea she saw a boat and, standing in the prow of the boat, a young man. He was dark, broad-shouldered, and slim and wore only a short striped skirt and a head-scarf of the same material. He was looking forward from his boat, but as she stared at the inward vision, the man turned and looked into Aurora's eyes. He smiled, and she thought she had never seen such merriment in a human face. His eyes crinkled and sparkled, and his teeth shone white as foam in the dark face. Then the vision vanished, and she felt her father's hand upon her shoulder.

3

THE family ate only once a day, shortly after midday. In the morning, on arising, they took hot water with some honey dissolved in it, and at night they drank a tea colored with saffron and herbs and made salty with a small measure of sea water. But the midday meal was sumptuous, a time when all the family and all the workers on the estate ate together, at long tables set out on the verandas.

There were flat loaves of bread made from barley and corn, and many dishes made of vegetables combined into savory stews flavored with garlic and onion and with wild leaves gathered from the hillsides. There were several kinds of cheeses made from milk of the white cows and of the little agile, skipping, black-and-white goats, and an abundance of fruits were piled at intervals on the tables. Pots of honey were set out, plus small jars of salt taken from the sea water.

Drako had been to the city and had returned with his four sons. He was an older, grizzled version of his stalwart boys. Ramo and Akil towered over him by almost eight inches, and both were very strong. Akil, especially, could perform outstanding feats of strength; he could lift great rocks and move enormous tree trunks. His father often said that he should have named him after the hero Hercules, who had known how to move mountains. Aram, shorter and slighter, wore the dark blue skirt and headscarf of a mariner; already he had been allowed to have a tattooed design on his left arm. When he was a master shipbuilder and had made a successful voyage, he could have Poseidon's trident bitten into his shoulder in bright colors, so that all the world could know his calling and his authority. Baka, small and sullen in expression, wore the brown skirt and headband of a student.

Drako, after he had his first taste of the warm bread and a piece of salty cheese, called to Baka, who sat at the lowest place in the family table because he was the youngest son, "Come, Baka, what marvels are you and your teachers up to now? I suppose you will be inventing chariots that fly through the air before long!"

Baka replied at once, "Who knows, Father? I might be. There were such chariots in ancient times."

"So they say," answered Drako thoughtfully. "But no one has ever found any bits or pieces of one or anything to prove that they ever existed."

"But," said Baka with his slightly superior smile, "if people remember that there were such things, then there must have been such things! The mind does not invent; it merely registers and remembers."

Drako looked at his son quizzically. "I have much to learn from you, I realize that," he commented softly, but Mara colored with annoyance. She had taught her children to be respectful at all times, and there was something in Baka's attitude that worried her.

Drako turned to Aram. Aram was his favorite, but at the meal he always addressed one of the younger sons first, for he was a very tender man and did not wish any of his children to know that Aram was first in his heart.

As a young man, Drako had wanted to learn shipbuilding and sailing, and the Council of Elders who ruled Poseida had given their consent, until his older brother, who was in charge of the family saffron fields, died in a sudden severe illness and Drako, as next of kin, was obliged to take over the cultivation of the sacred flower. So when Aram had turned his heart toward the sea, Drako helped him to realize his ambition and begin his studies.

"You asked what marvels we are up to," Baka said then. "I can't tell, for we are pledged to secrecy, but my teacher, Lakon, is working on an idea that will change the world."

Drako ate slowly, without further comment. Inwardly he was thinking: I must not challenge the boy. It is well that he have dreams and ideals of a better, a changed world. But I have heard many such plans, and sometimes, I know, there have been sudden changes, but man himself seems to change very little and his institutions are seldom any better than the men who constitute them.

Atlanta looked at her father, with eyes that seemed to tell him that she had heard his unvoiced thoughts in her mind. He smiled wryly, indicating that he did not think himself an authority on anything. Her answering smile was one of pure love.

But Baka had seen the small exchange of looks, and while he could not catch their thoughts, he sensed that they had to do with him, and he also divined a sort of criticism. This enraged him. Criticism, or opposition of any kind, unleashed a tormented sort of hatred in his heart. He made up his mind to get even before the day was over.

His chance came in the late afternoon when he saw that Aurora and Atlanta had gone for a swim in the cool water of the cove. It was low tide; waves curled lazily against the white sand, and there were no breakers, only softly heaving water. The twin girls sported and dived and shook their wet hair from their eyes. A dolphin came in near them and seemed to laugh and play with them, but when Baka waded into the water, the dolphin flipped himself under the water and disappeared.

Baka had brought with him from the laboratory in the city a white crystalline powder that had a curious property: once wet with sea water, it gave off a greenish gas that quickly overcame the mind, and put anyone who was near enough to breathe it into a deep sleep. Baka had intended to show this to his family and explain it, but he had been angered at dinner and he meant now to use the gas to confuse his sisters. Perhaps, he thought, Atlanta will speak while she is sleeping, and she may tell me some of her secrets.

Baka loved secrets and was always trying to penetrate the hidden places in the minds of his brothers and of his companions at the laboratory. It disturbed him sometimes that he himself had no secrets to tell and no confidant to share precious thoughts.

He had wrapped the crystals in a pouch of soft material that did not admit water. So, after diving under his sisters and pulling them down into the water with him (games that amused them and which they enjoyed), he waited until they were all tired and ready to leave the water and rest on the beach. Then, furtively, so that the girls should not see him, he opened the pouch and allowed the sea water to wet the crystals.

The girls had thrown themselves down, wet and glistening, upon the sand. Baka dropped down close to them both and passed the crystals, now giving off the pale green gas, under their noses. Before she lost consciousness, Aurora looked at him in hurt and bewilderment, but Atlanta only looked sad.

Baka had been afraid to let his sisters breathe too much of the sleep-inducing gas, but he had not realized that they would sleep so long. They lay unmoving, breathing deeply, for a long time, it seemed, and, to his disappointment, were silent. The tide had turned and was coming in, moving with more and more energy upward along the beach. When it had almost reached the girls, Baka had no choice but to move them back, and as he was doing this, Aram came along and watched him.

"What are you doing?" he asked. "What is the matter with the girls?"

Baka did not want to show the crystals; he was forced to shove the little pouch down into the sand, and then look up, with feigned innocence, at his brother.

"They're asleep," he said, "and the sea is coming close."

Aram lifted Aurora easily in his arms and carried her well away from the advancing waves. Baka, trying to emulate him, could not lift Atlanta. Shamed and frustrated, he had to wait for Aram to come and help him move her up to where Aram had laid Aurora on the grass. Atlanta turned her head and moaned.

"There is a strange smell," said Aram in a worried voice. "What is it?"

"Perhaps—perhaps—" began Baka, feeling an urge to confess what he had done.

But Atlanta opened her eyes. "Not important," she murmured, but she was looking at Baka. "Aurora will waken soon. It wasn't really important. But, Baka, you must not do these things. You must not."

"I don't know what you mean," he answered, hostile again and determined to come back and find the buried pouch in the sand so that no one could know of it.

I won't confess this, he thought. They'll forget it.

Aram was moving Aurora's arms, waking her.

"No," said Atlanta to Baka. "I won't forget. But I

don't hate you, Baka. Why do you think so? Why do you do these things?"

"I don't know what you mean," he mumbled again, not looking at her.

Aram helped the girls back to the house. Atlanta sent her twin a strong thought: let us not mention this. As their father came toward them on the veranda, they smiled.

"We got overtired," said Aurora, obediently.

4

SOME weeks later, Aurora and Atlanta finished sewing new dresses. They were made of very soft, fine material that clung to their young limbs and fell in the softest folds. Both girls wore shades of saffron, Aurora's a deep gold, Atlanta's pale as winter sunlight. Their sandals were tied with golden woven bands, and their hair was held back from their brows with round combs decorated with gold. They were going into the city with their parents, to witness one of the great Sea Spectacles.

Hesperidia was the center of learning and religion, and there were several temples, built with round towers, where the priestesses of the sea learned their duties, sang their prayers, and performed their rites.

The people of Poseida, living by the sea as they did,

measured time by the tides and referred to sections of time as parts of the tide. There was Tide one-eighth, then Tide one-sixth, and so on until they came to Tide One. Some also referred to sun time in the same way, as Sun one-eighth, Sun one-sixth, and so on, to Full Sun (which was noon), and thence downward, to Sundown. The Archers generally thought in tide times.

The Archers rose in the hour before dawn, to walk to the city. Walking swiftly, without stopping (and all were good walkers, swinging out freely and taking long steps, rising on the balls of their feet, moving their arms rhythmically), they would reach Hesperidia before the sun was high.

"Aram will be waiting for us at the docks," said Drako. "He expects us at Tide one-sixth."

A light soft mist rose from the sea; it made the girls' cheeks pink and brought out all the curl in their hair.

As the sun rose, glowing and fair, just beyond the mountains to the east, Hesperidia came into view. The city followed the natural curve of a sheltered bay, and from that bay the people had built a great curving canal which surrounded the city in a semicircle on the land side. Thus the city was entirely protected by sea water, for the tides rose and fell inside the canals, and the gentle scent of salt water hung over everything and mixed with the odors of flowers and fruits from the gardens. At intervals along the canal the round stone towers of the Sea Priestesses could be seen, with their long narrow windows let into the sides of the curving walls, through which the priestesses could see out but not be seen. Back, near the hills, were the schools and laboratories of the scientists.

A broad stone wall was built very high on the land side along the Great Canal, and steps led up to the top of the wall, which was some six feet broad and formed a fine pavement on which to walk. The Archers clambered up the wall and walked along it toward the bay, where Aram lived at the shipbuilding docks with his teachers.

As they walked, Aurora and Atlanta in front, their hands linked, they saw Aram. He came toward them, yodeling, and they could see that he was very happy to have them with him. He saluted his parents and his sisters and called, "I have a wonderful surprise today! Besides the Blessing of the Sea, a fine ship is coming in from Egypt! It should make port about two hours before sundown!"

Atlanta loved Aram. Like her, he felt the tides of the beloved sea rise and fall within his being, and he could not imagine life away from the sound of the water or the soft salt breath of the waves.

"Where are we to sit?" called Aurora. "You said you had splendid seats for us, where we could see everything."

"So I have," he answered. "Follow me now."

He strode ahead, leading them down off the canal wall and into a long low series of rooms built out over the bay. There were many young men, all wearing the same blue clothes as Aram and working at benches in those rooms; they all looked up and smiled at the passing party from outside the city.

In the last room, where two elderly men sat looking at plans on a high table, Aram stopped and bowed. "Honored Teachers, please meet my parents and my sisters."

One of the men was tall and thin, with a long, thoughtful face and a sweet smile. The other was short, brawny, and merry, with bright blue eyes. Both had tridents tattooed on their shoulders; they were master mariners and shipbuilders.

"We are pleased to see that you have arrived early," said the thin one. "Aram is the student who has won the greatest number of approbations this lunar month, so it was he who could have guests for the Sea Spectacle. We have a dais for you on the balcony; you will see everything. My name is Sind. I am to have the honor of sitting with you."

Introductions were made, and Sind led the Archers through a wide door and out onto an open balcony above the water. The canal here broadened and opened into the bay, and there was a sweeping view of the semicircle of the harbor right across to where the other canal and water gates could be seen. The great circular canal around Hesperidia sucked up the flow of water from the incoming tide through one end of the canal, while the other end was stopped by a great mechanical gate let down by machinery at the moment of the tide turn. When the ocean and the bay signaled that the tide was going out, the in-let gate came down and the canal waters rushed back into the sea with the receding tide and were carried far out. Thus the waters were never stagnant or filled with sand, and the wide canal could be navigated by boats of any size. At the same time, the city was perfectly guarded.

At fixed points along the canal and along the bay shore were small water-purification machines from which pipes carried pure drinking water into the homes.

The hollow, reverberating tones of great conch shells being blown echoed now over the city.

"They are coming!" cried Aurora, clasping her hands in excitement. Drums beat and the music of flutes and cymbals sounded.

Aram, sitting beside Aurora, told her, "The musicians lead the Sea Priestesses out into their boats now. The young men who blow the conchs must be very strong, for it takes skill and power to make the shells call out so loudly. And everyone must hear."

People were crowding the canal walls now, waiting for the ritual parade of boats. They began to come into view, moving slowly down the canal toward where the Archers sat, for the docks where Aram worked and studied were near the outward-tide gates of Hesperidia.

Atlanta watched with eyes made unusually observant, for not more than a dozen moons were to wax and wane before she joined the Sea Priestesses herself.

The boats were not large. Two priestesses sat on each bench, totaling ten, and one stood on a small elevation at the prow of each boat, and another at the stern. The boats were decorated with flowers and each priestess wore a garland of flowers and shells and a belt woven of small pearly shells held her robe close to her body. The robes were of a thin silky material, changing in color from blue to green and back again to blue as they moved.

Preceded by a boat carrying the musicians, the parade began. People along the sides of the canals shouted and cried, and some of them sang. They did not throw flowers or confetti, for it was strictly forbidden to throw anything into the sea canal, and anyone who did this was tried for the crime.

"Tell us about this rite," suggested Mara, who knew it, for she had watched it many times, but she wished her daughter Atlanta to have the pleasure of explaining it.

"There are many Sea Spectacles," answered Atlanta. "But two are the most important ones, the great ones of the year. The Spectacle of Life is the one we are seeing today. The priestesses row out beyond the bay into the sea and make obeisance to the Great Waters and thank the Sea Spirit for the gift of life. This spectacle takes place at the time of the full moon in the spring of the year, when all the plants of the earth begin to show the force of their life and growing. The other great ritual is the Spectacle of Death, when the Sea Priestesses thank the waters for taking us back into the great eternal spirit, one by one, as we are called."

"I have never let you watch that one," murmured Mara.

Aurora spoke. "Is it because you are afraid that the Eternal Spirit might call us if we watch, Mother?"

"Partly this. It is not the custom to let the young people watch the Spectacle of Death. It is very sad. But also —the priestesses always choose one of their number to give to the waters then, as a symbol of obedience."

"How do they choose that priestess?" asked Aurora.

"She volunteers," said Atlanta. "It is a great honor."

Atlanta spoke calmly, but Aurora shivered suddenly in the warm sunlit air.

The boats of the priestesses passed by, gliding smoothly on the water. As they proceeded out into the bay, the boats dipped and swung, for a smart breeze had sprung up and whitecaps began to show, like snowflakes, against the blue water.

"Do the boats never capsize?" asked Drako. "Where the bay widens into the sea water, the waves will be large and rough."

"They are well-balanced and weighted," said Aram. "We build them, and there are many secrets in the construction, to make them seaworthy. They always come back safely from the great waters beyond the bay."

When the last of the boats had passed out of sight onto the broad bosom of the sea waters beyond Hesperidia's bay, the people opened their lunch baskets and passed around their refreshments. Mara had brought barley loaves sweetened with honey and filled with raisins and nuts, chunks of salty cheese, juicy fresh fruits, and a cool drink brewed from the toasted berries of a wild bush that grew on the mountainsides.

"I am sorry Ramo and Akil could not come," murmured Atlanta.

"We must never leave the sacred flowers untended," reminded her mother.

"Why didn't you invite Baka?" asked Aurora.

"The students at the laboratory on the hillside can see everything even better than we here at the shore," explained Aram. "They have great glasses they look into which show everything to them, larger than life and perfectly clear, no matter how far away. He would not have wanted to sit here with us."

They talked and moved about, in and out of the study rooms, until the boats bearing the priestesses returned from sea on the rising tide.

"How do they guide the boats?" wondered Aurora.

"They are guided by a magnetic machine which the priestesses own; they tell us it was brought down to them from heaven by an angel," explained Aram. "As for us, we study the tides and the stars and the sun, and guide our ships with special machines only when the winds fail us or when they are going in a different direction from where we want to go."

Far up on the hillside, within the towers of the science laboratory where Baka was a student, the masters sat before a large polished crystal of glass, in which appeared everything that was happening down at the port. The students had been allowed to watch with them as the priestesses put out to sea in their decorated crafts, but when the boats were no longer visible the students had been sent back to their quarters. Baka, however, pretended to have turned his ankle at the door of the crystal room, and so they let him stay. He massaged his ankle and swayed and moaned to give credence to his deceit, but surreptitiously he watched the wonderful crystal, focusing on a corner of the picture which appeared on it, and thus he was able to watch his sisters, his parents, and Aram.

With a kind of pleasure mixed with pain and jealousy, he watched. He admired Aram, he loved him, and he envied him. With bitterness in his heart, he watched his father with Aram; he sensed the deep comradeship, the affection between them.

But I am the most brilliant one in the family, thought Baka, full of resentment. Aram will be nothing but a sailor; there are dozens of them. I will be a scientist, a master scientist, and only ten of us are chosen from all Poseida every five years! Yet my father never dropped his arm over my shoulders that way, and my sisters don't lean against me and look up at me like that!

Baka's longings were clouded by his egotism and envy; deep in his heart, he would have given anything to be the son as warmly loved as Aram. Slowly his hot jealousy and anger cooled; slowly he strengthened himself with cool and precise plans for his own advancement. The seed of a plan to make himself powerful took root in his heart. With it went the thought: If they will not love me, they shall fear me.

Limping and favoring his ankle, he left, and when the students were called back into the crystal room to watch the return of the boats from the sea, he remained in his room, pretending to be weary.

5

ARAM'S teachers had provided a resting place for
the ladies of Aram's family, and there Mara and
her daughters sat on cushions and dozed, or whispered,
until the afternoon sun was sinking and the boats came
back to shore, proceeding through the other canal gate.

"It was lovely," sighed Atlanta. "Such a beautiful day!
Thank you, Aram."

"The day is not over!" cried her brother. "Don't you
remember? The Egyptian boat will be making port in a
little while. Look! I see the tip of a sail just there, on the
horizon."

Aram's eyes were keen and far-seeing. He had dis-
cerned the sail before the others, but after some minutes
all the family saw the red-and-black-striped canvas loom-

ing larger, and then they saw the boat, slim and long, painted black, as it cut and skimmed through the waves. It came swiftly and made for the docks below Aram's study house.

Soon the girls saw the figure of a young man in the prow, and Aurora gasped. It was the young man of her dream, wearing the red-and-black-striped short skirt and head-scarf of the Egyptian sailors, and as she looked, he saw Aram standing on the balcony, looked up at him, and lifted his brown arm in greeting. White teeth flashed in his dark face.

It is he, it is he, thought Aurora.

"That is my friend Set," said Aram. "He is an Egyptian captain, a very fine sailor, and we have had good talks. May I invite him to come home with us?"

"Please do," said Mara.

"He will be welcome," added Drako.

The family did not remain to meet the young Egyptian mariner, for Mara wished to get home early and check on the saffron in the drying rooms. It worried her to be away all day, though her sons Ramo and Akil were careful and devoted. So, after farewells and thanks, the Archers started back toward their home.

Despite the glare of the sinking sun, the walk was pleasurable, for the tide was coming in along the shore, and with it a cool wind, full of the fresh breath of the sea. As they came in view of their lands, the two girls started to run, and the parents looked at them fondly and proudly as they skimmed along the path, their hair flying, their long, clean limbs flashing. Laughing and gasping for breath, Atlanta and Aurora reached their own veranda and threw themselves down upon it to rest.

When they could speak to each other, Aurora said, "I wonder when Aram will bring the Egyptian captain."

"Day after tomorrow," answered Atlanta. "I just now caught their thoughts; they are talking and making arrangements. Wait—" She threw back her head and seemed to be listening, but slowly a flush mounted from her throat and stained her face a deep rose.

"What is it?" demanded Aurora. "What are they saying?"

"Oh, things men say," answered Atlanta, not looking at her. "I shan't listen any more."

The two young men had gone to the baths and were once more dressed.

"I am hungry," announced Set. "We Egyptians eat in the evening—not like you Poseidans, who stuff yourselves at midday! That's because we must work during the hours of light, and food makes the brain sleepy!"

Aram knew his friend's custom of teasing and joking; Set never seemed serious unless he was at the prow of his ship. Then his concentration was keen, and nothing distracted him.

Aram took Set with him to one of the seaside restaurants which served meals, along an avenue that faced the bay. As the sun sank, they sat at a table before steaming dishes of vegetables spiced with various herbs, and bowls of thick sour milk and cream made savory with spices and aromatic leaves. For dessert they were served platters of fresh fruits.

"You will eat well at my home," promised Aram. "When can you come to visit us?"

"I have business to settle here tomorrow, but I could come the day after," offered Set. "And I would like to," he went on, looking almost shyly at his friend. "I will tell you frankly, I have fallen in love with your sister. I never saw such a beautiful girl!"

"But they are both beautiful," protested Aram, setting down his piece of wheat bread. "And they look exactly alike. We can scarcely tell them apart!"

"But," Set went on in a puzzled tone, "I mean the one in the very pale yellow dress. She has an aura around her, a lovely blue—not like the sea, but reminding me of it; not like heaven, but near it."

"The one in the pale yellow dress is Atlanta," said Aram slowly, "and she is promised to be a priestess of the sea."

Set looked stricken. "So I have set my heart on a priestess," he murmured. "What bad luck for me! Would she change her mind?"

Aram shook his head. "Don't try to change her, Set. Besides, she feels a devotion for what will be her life. And my mother promised her."

Set sighed. "Well, so be it," he murmured, and ate for a time in silence.

"Aurora is lovely, too," said Aram later. Then Set looked at him with his sudden flashing smile, his look of mischief. "Is that so? I shall remember to notice, day after tomorrow. Is she promised to someone?"

"Not yet."

"Well."

The two young men strolled in the twilight and later went on board Set's boat, where Aram had permission to spend the night. As they leaned against the rail around the top deck watching the stars wheel into place in the dark sky, Set said, "There are no women in my family. We are five men. My mother has always wanted a daughter. She will cherish my bride, when I choose one."

Aram smiled. "Would she cherish a foreigner? We Poseidans have many colonies overseas and we have sent our rulers to preside and govern. Poseidans are not always loved. Your family is Egyptian."

"Egypt is the friend of Poseida, as of all Atlantis," said Set bluntly. "We were originally one of the colonies, as you know, and we treasure our Atlantean heritage."

"I had to hear you say it—before I take you to my home," said Aram.

The two young men struck hands suddenly, understanding each other very well.

6

ON the day of Aram's visit with Set, Atlanta saw that Aurora had chosen a pale blue gown to wear, so she went to choose another color and settled on a soft beige, the very hue of her tanned skin.

"Oh, don't wear that old dress," protested Aurora. "We are to have a guest. Dress in blue, like me."

"No," said Atlanta gently. "I want you to be especially lovely today, and the blue suits you best. Besides, I plan to work among the flowers, and my fingers will be stained from the pistils of the saffron. I will be so busy—and perhaps so stained and spotted—that I may not eat dinner with the family at all. Do not look for me."

Aurora regarded her sister. "I will feel shy without you —the only woman of the family, besides Mother."

"You will have much to ask the young guest," said Atlanta. "He is a captain and must have seen great marvels. You won't miss me." And she went away swiftly to help in the plucking rooms.

Work had already begun, and the women of the families who lived on Archer land were already singing, to give rhythm to their busy hands. The harvest of flowers was heavy, and carts drawn by cattle came in from the fields constantly. Men were to be seen throughout the fields, replanting the bulbs taken from the first harvest, for the flowers, though they would bloom from the same plant for several crops, flourished better and grew stronger if the bulbs were regularly lifted from the earth, cleansed, and set back in a different place, in earth that had been turned and lifted and softened and mulched with the wet leaves of the sacrificed plants from which the flowers had been taken.

Drako was always careful to give back to the earth what he took from it, and every year he ceremoniously buried, in his plots of land, enough of the pistils from the flowers to show the earth that he would not rob her entirely of her bounty. He did the same with fruits from his trees and wheat and barley from his fields.

Akil, the second youngest son, the tallest and strongest of all, was in charge of the mill which made flour of the wheat and barley. He was a quiet boy, and because of his great shoulders and strong arms, his slow way of talking, and his shyness, some people supposed that he was not as bright as he might be. He stood much in awe of Baka, his brilliant younger brother. But Akil was inventive in his own way and he had devised a scheme by which the sea would help turn the stones of the mill. He had built, with his own hands, a deep canal into which sea water rushed at high tide. This he directed over a small precipice he had constructed from stones, whence it fell into a pond and then found its way out and back into the sea again. The rushing water turned a wheel that moved the grinding stones against each other, and the flour fell away and was stored in sacks in a small dry stone house, which Akil kept in good repair.

Today several women of the families who worked with the Archers came for their weekly allotments of flour, and Akil, his short skirts and headband all powdery, weighed out their shares on scales that his father had given him.

"You are a good boy, Akil," said one woman, who was old and did not work among the flowers any more, for Drako felt that only young fingers should deal with the delicate blooms. Besides, every family needed one woman at home, to watch over the little ones and nurse the sick. "You never give short measure."

"Why would anyone do that?" asked Akil, puzzled.

"Oh, I have worked on other lands where it was tried," answered the old woman. She had a leathery, lined face, but had all her teeth, and her eyes were as bright as those of any young woman. "There are sometimes people who want to take advantage of others."

"But why?" asked Akil. "Right is right, and fair is fair."

"Because there are people in Poseida who are vain and jealous and want to hold power over others," she said. "You have not far to look for one of them."

Akil made no answer, but he began unhappily pondering what the old woman could mean. He ran after her as she started away, down the seaside path lined with pink sand flowers. "Tell me, please," he asked, "what you mean. Has someone on these lands cheated you? Do you have some complaint which you should take before my father?"

The old woman turned and looked at him thoughtfully. The sea breeze lifted her graying hair and tugged softly at her dark green dress and striped apron. "There is no one here at present," she said at last, "who does these things. But you are a guileless young man, and good. Take my warning. Do not trust everyone."

Akil returned thoughtfully to the mill and kept turning the words of the old woman over and over in his mind. He did not like the conclusion he came to and decided to keep his own counsel until he had made up his mind what to do.

Thus, Akil at his mill, worried over a problem, and Atlanta in the plucking room, determined to keep herself out of sight of the Egyptian, did not appear at the family table. Mara and Drako were upset at the vacant places and asked pardon of the young mariner. But he bowed so respectfully, his smile and his words were so simple and winning, that they ceased to be annoyed at the absence of their children.

Ramo greeted Set and said, "I can show you about our lands and take you for an afternoon swim at our beach. It would be my pleasure."

"I would enjoy that," answered Set. "And also I would like very much to see your saffron-processing rooms. I bring an order for a shipload of the pressed saffron, if you have that much to sell."

Drako began to measure out large glasses of mint tea that had been cooled with cubes from a machine he owned which changed fluid water quickly into squares of iridescent ice. He turned courteously to his guest. "I myself will take you through our drying rooms and the plucking and packing rooms," he offered. "And we can discuss your purchase. You realize that I must get the consent of the Elders to sell any of the sacred flower."

"I know," said Set. He sat cross-legged and ate with good appetite but neatly and fastidiously. Aurora, stealing glances at him from under her long eyelashes, saw only things to admire about the stranger: his brown arms and slim-fingered, strong hands; his thin compact waist, no larger around than her own; his dark eyes, set under brows that arched upward toward where his hair, blue-black and glistening, shone under the scarlet head-band.

"I will be glad to wait upon the Elders with you," went on Set—and Aurora approved of his deep voice, even of his rough Egyptian accent, as he used the Atlantean words—"to explain that it is the priests of our temples who wish to make the purchase, and their purpose is to use the saffron to dye their holy garments—nothing else." And Aurora saw that Set had a round black mole underneath one eye, and another near his mouth, which seemed to her to give him a droll and endearing expression, especially when he smiled, which was frequently.

The ladies retired after the meal, and Drako and his sons and Set rested on the veranda for a while, watching the sea, and then Drako proposed that they all visit the rooms in which the saffron was processed. The strong aromatic scent of the sacred flower came to them as they drew near the long line of buildings where the work was done.

"First, the plucking rooms," said Drako. "We have here only young girls, with quick light fingers, so as to bruise the delicate pistil the least and maintain all the rich pollen upon it."

As they entered the room, where the scent was almost overpowering, Set suddenly stood still. And Atlanta, her hands almost dark brown with the stain, looked up and seemed frozen also—gray-green eyes looking deeply into black eyes.

"But what are you doing here?" Drako asked his daughter. He was displeased that she had not attended luncheon with the family.

"I came to help, and I lost track of the hour," she said, dropping her eyes.

"The others can manage without you," said her father shortly. "Go and bathe and dress; we have a guest."

"Yes, Father." Atlanta rose to her feet at once and, with bowed head, glided away.

Drako led the young men through the older rooms,

explaining the processes and taking a great deal of care to show how fine weights were used to measure each packet of the dried and bricked saffron, so that every one was equal to every other.

"And we never pack the slightest sliver of straw or grass or any other thing in our saffron bricks," went on Drako proudly. "We have had the honor of being the largest cultivators of saffron since my great-grandfather's time, and we are very proud of our record for absolute integrity, and the purity of our saffron."

Set seemed to come to himself and was able to pay attention to the weighing of the saffron bricks and the packing of the finished product, though visions of a lovely startled face, under a saffron-stained headband, were haunting him.

Aram and Set planned to go back to Hesperidia by sea, and the tide would not be right for them until two hours after dark; thus they returned to the veranda and sat about talking and drinking some honey-sweetened tea at sundown. Atlanta, shiningly clean and dressed in a short pale-green gown, served the tea and moved quietly among the people seated on the veranda.

"Could we take a walk?" suggested Set as the breeze from the sea began to blow in toward them. "It is such a pleasant hour."

"Let's!" Aram, Ramo, and Akil stood up, eager to be off and to show Set their caves, where the incoming tide rushed through with a roar and sometimes made other sounds, weird singing noises and hisses and eerie calls.

"The girls, too," shouted Aram. "Let's all go!"

They started out briskly, walking along the sea path. Akil wanted Set to see the mill, and they all turned down toward where Akil had built his canal, his water-drop, and the stone warehouse. Somehow, as they regrouped to walk down to where the arches could be seen, Set managed to be walking alongside Atlanta. Aurora walked ahead with Aram.

"I have been longing to talk to you," began Set impulsively.

Atlanta looked up at him. "I know."

"I wish we could be friends," he plunged on. Ramo and Akil were ahead, with Aram and Aurora.

"But we are," said Atlanta. "I will be your friend."

"I mean—I wish we could be more than friends. I want—I would like to ask permission to court you," Set went on in a thick voice, taking her hand. "I have never seen a girl as lovely as you. I cannot get you out of my thoughts."

Atlanta smiled. "I am flattered," she said gently. "But I am not to be courted. I have been promised to the Great Ocean. I shall serve it, just as you do. I am to be a Sea Priestess."

"Oh," he cried, "cannot that be changed? You are not yet one of them. Please, do not join the priestesses."

"But I have already joined them in my heart. And besides, my mother promised me."

The young Egyptian looked stricken to the heart and Atlanta was moved to lay her other hand atop his.

"Don't grieve about me," she said softly. "I will watch over you and pray for you and ask the Great Ocean to keep you safe always."

Then she took her hand away. "Come, the others are getting ahead of us," she said. Set followed her, heavy-hearted.

7

AFTER the young men had left, pushing Aram's light homemade boat out into the sea and unfurling a sail which the breeze took at once, turning them toward Hesperidia, the sisters went to their sleeping quarters. It was a lovely night, with a full moon, and Aurora was sleepless. She wanted to talk, especially about the visitor.

"How long will it take them to make the bay of Hesperidia?"

"A short time, less than half the time it took us to walk. They have the tide and the wind with them. The sea will carry them safely."

"I like him, Aram's friend," Aurora said shyly. "Don't you think him handsome?"

"Yes, I do," answered Atlanta. "And he is good. A good man. I could hope that you might marry one like him some day."

Aurora blushed, glad that the darkness would not show her hot cheeks to her sister. But Atlanta had been feeling very sensitive all day and could read the thoughts near her and even some that were being sent toward her from far away.

"Well," began Aurora. "Well . . ."

"He is not married. Or promised," said Atlanta. "And I think he would be proud to unite himself with this family. And I," she added, putting her arms around Aurora, "I would like to think of you living somewhere far away —somewhere safe. Egypt will be safe."

"Oh," laughed Aurora, "you are getting morbid again! You are having those terrible visions. Cleanse your mind of them. Just as you always tell me to do when I lie down to sleep. Cleanse your mind. Let a soft sweet darkness drift before your closed eyelids."

"Yes," sighed Atlanta. "Come. Lie down. We must both sleep. Tomorrow is another day."

8

UP at the laboratory on the hill, the pupils were listening to a lecture by the Science Master, Lakon. He had grown old in the service of science, had never married, and was thought to have no human relations. He was short and very fair, with prominent blue eyes, and as he would tolerate no hair upon his body but shaved face and head, arms and legs to keep himself glistening smooth, nobody could tell his age. The story among the pupils was that Lakon was twice as old as any living man on Atlantis. It was even said that he had seen the famous air chariots that had once raced through the clouds, although the secret for conducting them by means of the sun's energy and the magnetism of the earth had been forgotten. This could not have been true, for Lakon was still vigorous, erect, and full-fleshed. He was taciturn, however, and very strict with the pupils, and no one loved him. For this reason, they made up stories about him and speculated about him, ascribing to him more technical knowledge and less wisdom than he actually had.

Lakon did not stand while the pupils sat, as was customary in some of the classes in the laboratory. He reversed this. He sat, sometimes even lolling, and he required that the pupils remain standing and at attention.

"I have heard it said," he began in his rather high, penetrating voice—and, as he spoke, his light keen eyes traveled from face to face among the students, noting their reactions—"that I have seen the flying chariots of old. I have not. However, I have devoted my life to research upon what could have been the propulsion factor in those chariots. For I am one of the scientists—there are not many of my company, I confess—who believe that they did exist and that our forebears colonized not only the nearby coasts but far across the Great Ocean on the other side of the world, traveling in air ships.

"Be that as it may. I am now at a point in my studies where I must select some helpers, for I believe I have come upon the principle which our ancient and far more civilized ancestors used. In a word, it is a concentration of the sun's energy into a small, very hard crystal which can be made to hoard and treasure up this energy. Once the crystal has absorbed all the energy that can be directed into it, the problem is how to hold it and then how to release it, on demand, in measured amounts. I need hardly point out that this crystal, once we begin our actual work, must be guarded night and day, and also that the secret of the procedure must be kept absolutely.

"Indeed, I have spoken with the Elders and we have agreed that, for the safety of mankind, anyone who betrays the secret of the work we are about to embark upon will be put to death, and summarily. We cannot even risk a trial, for that might spread the news, and disquietude and panic would result. Therefore"—here Lakon rose and stared intently at each of the ten pupils before him—"be warned."

Baka began to tremble uncontrollably and his jaw shook like that of a small cat which is hunting. He felt tremendously elated, thrilled. Rushing to his mind was a longing to tell about being a part of this wonderful scientific study which would result in amazing power.

The one who owns that crystal, he thought, could control the world.

"Whoever owns the crystal," Lakon went on, "will be able to wield great power. For good or evil. And since it *must* be for good, we must guard it with our very lives. Is there anyone here who is not willing to obligate himself thus far?"

No answer. All the students were overcome with excitement and with awe at the prospect of the work before them.

"Good," said Lakon dryly after a time. "For if any one of you had revealed that he was *not* willing, he would have had to sleep in the cellar room this night."

A shiver passed over the young men. The cellar room

was a small stone sleeping apartment into which an odorless, colorless, tasteless gas could be admitted, causing the sleeper to die peacefully. It was used in extreme cases, when the Elders and the master scientists agreed that some pupil would be unworthy or unreliable if released into the world armed with the special knowledge of the science schools.

"We will form teams," went on Lakon, "and these teams will work with me for three moons each, never leaving the laboratory at any time during those three moons. Every one of you will be associated with me in this work, and it may take us years to finish. Remember, absolutely sealed lips whenever you are outside the laboratory. Now I will choose the first team. And the work will begin."

He was silent for a moment, thinking and considering. At last he made up his mind.

"I will have Socha." He indicated a tall boy who was the best in the class at mathematics. "And Baka."

Baka fell to the floor in a dead faint.

Lakon looked down upon him with a smile and then gently raised him.

"Baka," he said, "I hesitated, for I have often felt that you have not entirely left the world behind but have some material ambitions of the sort we cannot tolerate here. But I see that your joy at being chosen to work with me overcame your senses. I am pleased."

II

1

THE year went by.

Baka was seldom able to come home, but when he was home Mara was pleased with him, for he no longer answered his father with disrespectful carelessness or played tricks on his sisters or Akil. He was thoughtful and quiet.

Atlanta and Aurora grew in grace and loveliness, and Aram received the tattoo of the sailor's star. In another year he would receive the trident, and then he would be allowed to build and sail his own ship.

Set made two voyages from Egypt, each time with orders to purchase saffron, and the orders were approved by the Elders. Each time Set arrived, Atlanta would arrange to be very busy somewhere indoors, in her home or about the processing rooms of the sacred flower.

So it was that Set began to notice Aurora and to seek her company. At first he meant only to guide the conversation to Atlanta and ask about her. Aurora accepted his interest guilelessly and frankly answered his occasional questions about her twin. Set, in love, felt a combination of emotions: he realized that Atlanta was not for him, and yet he rebelled at her acceptance of what he thought of as her "fate."

One day, when he had come to the Arches to spend the day, he and Aurora and Aram went to bathe in midafternoon. Some seals had come in to make their home in the cove, and the little sleek creatures cavorted playfully, smacking their tails on the water to make a loud sound and then diving at once.

Set was much diverted watching them. "I have seen the dolphins playing about the ship when I was at sea, but I have never seen the seals so close to shore and to people," he said to Aurora.

"They come for Atlanta," she said. "She attracts all the animals of the sea, as if they knew that she is to be a priestess. Besides the seals, dolphins often come here and swim about and wait for her. And so do the sea birds."

Some gulls arose, giving their hoarse cry, from rocks near the cove.

"And perhaps they come for you, too," Set said. "Couldn't that be so?"

"Maybe," agreed Aurora. "Because I love them so

much. But it is only Atlanta who can touch and caress them and talk with them."

"Talk—converse with them?"

"Oh yes. All the animals talk to Atlanta. She is more angel than human," she said softly. "We were born sisters, and born alike, but she has been chosen for some path I could never follow."

Set looked at Aurora with new eyes, noting the gentle unselfishness of her attitude, and her humility.

"I thought, when I first saw her," confessed Set, "that she walked in a cloud of shining blue light—an aura."

"You saw truly. She does. It is not always visible to everyone. The priestesses saw it at once when Mother took her to visit them as a child. They patted me on the head and gave me candy and nuts, but it was Atlanta they wanted for their own."

"And you never resented this?"

"Oh yes!" cried Aurora. "I did. Because I don't want to lose her! It is very hard to give her up and know that we won't be close any more—sharing a room, sharing dreams, secrets, imaginings. I love her."

Set drew a long breath. "And so do I," he told Aurora.

She looked at his profile, set in lines of youthful desperation, as he stared out at sea.

"Oh, don't grieve," she said. "At least you can always love her, and know that she will never belong to any other man."

"How sweet you are!" he said, turning fondly toward her.

Aurora flushed but made no answer. There was a sharp pain in her chest, but it could not be jealousy of Atlanta, she knew. She loved her too much. What was it, then?

2

O N the longest day of the year, Drako always gave a great feast for all the workers in the fields and in the drying rooms and spoke about the history of their country.

Nothing was spared to make this day one of great rejoicing and good fellowship. The families who lived near the Archers and worked with the sacred blossoms were gentle, good people, and Drako found many brilliant youngsters among them. These he educated in the city, and he saw to it that they were prepared for work in the profession or craft for which they seemed to have special gifts.

Long tables were set out in the shadow of the verandas. Mara and her daughters had been working for several days preparing all the delicate dishes that would be served. Mara herself made all the sauces and supervised the baking of bread and cakes. Aurora prepared the vegetables and fruits, and Atlanta made all the sweets, most of them with a base of honey, almonds, walnuts, and fruits, but some with the juice of a plant that Set had brought, which was now being grown in the farthest fields. The plant grew in tall canes, and inside these was a delicious sweet juice which could be boiled down and then dried, forming powdery crystals.

Atlanta had experimented with this and had found ways to combine it with milk and fruits and nuts and with the petals of various fragrant flowers, among them roses and violets, and she had invented some beautiful as well as delicious sweets.

Her success had elated her, for the priestesses of the sea supported their needs by selling some of their special products, such as perfumed candles; measures for time made of arrangements of colored water in glasses that tipped, dropping the water from one vessel into another, thus marking out the day into portions; embroideries and weavings; and shell paintings, which they made by gathering shells and gluing them to various wooden forms in delicate combinations of color. Atlanta now thought that she might be able to sell the sweets she was inventing with the juice of the plant, which Set told her had come from very far away, on the other side of the world, and was called Shu-car.

Akil and Ramo had planned some entertainment for the children of the families who worked with the Archers, and one of these was a boat ride through the arches and into some caves which at certain times of the day glowed with mysterious color. One cave showed a most wonderful deep blue which painted the water, the walls of the caves, and even the hands, faces, and clothes of anyone inside, with a magical light. Another cave gave off a color between violet and pink, entrancingly beautiful as it danced upon the waves. Still another glowed with a green that was both bright and deep.

The children were never allowed near the caves, for the sea rushed in to fill them to the brim when the tide was high and sucked the water out with great force at the ebb. There was a time when it was safe to enter the caves, but it was necessary to watch and calculate very carefully, for this time varied a little day by day. Akil and Ramo knew the tides and the hours, and they were going to show the caves after the feast, for on this day the safe time to visit would fall about two and a half hours before sunset.

All the workers and their families came in festive dress, wearing garlands of flowers around their shoulders and woven as crowns on their hair. None wore saffron: the deep gold of the saffron flower was used only by the Archer family and by persons dedicated to religious activities. But there were dresses in lavender and rose, in blue, pink, white, and green. A few men wore red, but it was not a popular color for dress, being associated with foreigners. The Egyptians who came to Poseida in their ships wore red, black, and rust-brown and, often, striped cottons in all these dark colors. The Atlanteans did not care for these; and no one wore black. Black being a kind of denial of light, they avoided it, for the Atlanteans were children of the light, and some even called themselves thus.

As soon as all the people had gathered and had greeted Drako and Mara, who awaited them on the veranda with goblets of fruit refreshments, a chorus of children began to sing Atlantean songs and the young people formed into circles and squares to dance. The music was supplied by some of the older men, who played for them on flutes and drums and on stringed instruments that were held under the arm and plucked, giving a splendid resonance and melody to the music.

The dancing and singing went on all during the feasting. Aurora, Atlanta, and their helpers were indefatigable, bringing dish after dish, succulent, fragrant with herbs and garlic and onions, or delicately perfumed with spices from lands to the east. Set had brought gifts of a dark-brown bark which, when powdered, gave a delicious taste to rice boiled in milk and to cakes made of barley flour, and a hot bitter pod that lent unexpected flavor to stewed vegetables and burned the mouth in a pleasurable way.

When at last everyone was satisfied, and even the children could eat no more, Drako rose and began the speech he made year after year.

"Dear friends and co-workers," he said. "Let us give thanks for all our blessings, and let us send our thoughts backward through Time to the Great Ones who were our

ancestors and who made Atlantis and Poseida our
mother country.

"Our great hero was Poseidon, who came to be known
as Lord of the Sea. He was one of the first Atlantean
heroes to lead groups of colonizers out from Atlantis to
other lands, and because he knew the seas and the Great
Ocean loved him and protected him, he is always shown
with a trident and is worshipped as a Hero-God. It was
Poseidon, too, who brought us the animals that give us
their milk and from which we make our cheeses and but-
ter. The first pair he brought us, he had himself taken
captive in one of the colonized lands of the inner seas.
Our girls and boys still celebrate this gift from Poseidon
by the Bull Games, which are allowed only on the day we
celebrate the memory of Poseidon, for the games are
dangerous and we have long since decided against any
entertainments that involve bloodshed. Only the most
skillful of our young bull dancers—student priests from
one of the great temples in the interior of this island—
are allowed to give the exhibitions. Their art is remarkable, as those of you who have been privileged to see
them know, and they have been sent to one of our colonies to teach this dance to other young priests."

Aurora listened to her father with love and respect.
She thought he might indeed have posed for a statue of
Poseidon himself, so broad and strong was he, his head
with thick graying hair so noble; his eyes, under heavy
brows, so calm and dominant; his beard so venerable.

Mara, tired from the previous days' work, sat in a kind

of trance. She had not eaten heavily, for she was disturbed about the plan to take the children into the caves; she had always distrusted the caves, with their unnatural light, and feared for her sons when they visited them. She ate a peach slowly and prayed intensely to the Great Ocean to hold his wrath and not harm any of the young ones.

Atlanta, too, had eaten little, for she was weary. Her thoughts strayed to Set, who had brought her gifts and had tried in every way he knew to persuade her to change the path she had chosen, the path she was destined for. She thought of him with affection, even with longing. He was the kind of young man she most admired, brave and resourceful, intelligent, but merry and delighted with all life's gifts.

He is sensitive and he will turn to Aurora soon, she thought. Especially after I enter the sisterhood, which will be soon now. He will love her more and more as time goes by. And I need him. He is to play an important part in my plan, when the day comes that I must act.

And, seeing visions of the future, she became sorrowful.

3

R A M O and Akil, looking at the sun, decided that they could enter the Caves of Light successfully. As they could not take all the children—there were about thirty in all, sons and daughters of the families who lived and worked on the Archer estate—the two great sunburned sons of Drako made the children line up and draw lots. Six could go in the boat and then, if there was time enough, another six. No more.

There was laughter and pushing and shouting as the young people, of all ages, formed a line and passed by Ramo, who held out a basket into which he had put thirty-odd straws of different colors. There were twelve blue straws, and those who drew the blue straws were chosen for the excursions. Akil stood near to blindfold each child before he reached into the basket to draw his straw.

As soon as the lucky twelve had drawn—leaping about with joy to know that they were to see the magical caves —Ramo and Akil divided them into two groups and took the first group rapidly down to the shore, where their boat was beached. It was a simple broad rowboat, and with Ramo and Akil at the oars, it sped across the heaving water swiftly and almost soundlessly.

Mara watched anxiously from the shore. But the boatload of children came back safely, and all were entranced, their small faces reflecting the wonder and joy of bathing in the strange, magical light of the caves.

"Are you sure you have time for the second group?" Mara asked.

"Oh, yes!" cried Ramo, looking at the sun, and the boat started out on a second journey.

But this time they did not return in the time allotted, and Mara began to wring her hands. "Drako, please go. And take some men with you. Something has happened."

Atlanta came running down to the beach, her face white and strained, but she said, "Be calm, Mother. They will all come back, and safely! Wait. Wait a moment." She seemed to stare into space, as if listening. Then she smiled and said, "Look now! Here they come."

And the boat appeared at the mouth of the cave of violet light. The water had risen very high and all the children were lying down so that the boat would be able to pass under the narrowed cave mouth. Ramo and Akil had left the boat and were swimming alongside it. Ramo at one end and Akil at the other, they propelled the boat back to shore and helped all the little ones out onto the dry sand.

Ramo looked quite crestfallen, and said to his father, "I had forgotten the whirlpool tide that forms in the Green Cave just before the water closes the entrance. It took our oars from our hands. I am ashamed."

"No matter. All are safe!" cried Mara. "Thank you, Great Ocean, for sparing our little ones. Thank you."

Atlanta, as if she heard a voice calling her, waded straight out into the water and lifted it with her hands in a gesture of love and humility. She was giving thanks, too, in her way.

The children had thought it all a great adventure and were excited and happy. Akil heard them chattering to their parents: "And Ramo was so angry when the witch of the Green Cave took the oars away from him and swallowed them! It was Akil who said, 'Get out, Ramo. We must swim with the boat and push it through the entrance, quickly! Quickly!'"

The music of the revelers started up again, and some of the boys and girls began to dance.

But Akil waited for Atlanta to emerge from the sea. He took her hand and placed it on his forehead. "I heard you," he whispered to her. "You told me what to do to save the little ones. We might all have gone down into the whirlpool!"

"Is there a way we could make the caves safer?" she asked. "You are clever at persuading the sea to obey you, to rush into canals and grind the stones of your mill together. We must think of some way. Take me tomorrow into the caves. I want to see them again."

"I must make new oars."

"Then as soon as you can! I want to see the colors again—before I go. You know that several moons from now I must leave. I must begin my work."

"I will take you into the caves—but carefully, by myself. Ramo is a man of the land, a planter of seeds, a harvester. I am a miller, yes, but I am a man of the sea. We understand each other. If it were not for Aram, who is to be our captain, I would have gone to sea myself."

"I know. But one day, one day you will be a great man of the sea, and people will remember you!" she promised him.

He smiled tenderly. He loved Atlanta and had great respect for her prophecies. Most of all, he depended on her, for she could send her thoughts to him. She had done this from their earliest childhood, saving him from many boyish dangers. Once, when he had gone exploring in the hills, he had heard her warning and had stopped still, just as a great snake had slithered across the path in front of him. Another time she had called to him sharply to look up, and he had seen a rock hurtling down upon him from the hillside and was able to get out of its way.

Atlanta was conscious of her power and never used it except in moments of emergency.

4

A K I L and Atlanta chose a bright calm day during the next full moon to visit the caves. The quiet moment when the tide was running out, but just before the incoming pull of the waves had begun, was the perfect moment for entering the Blue Cave.

Akil gave the boat a strong push with his oar, and it slid through the opening into a world Atlanta remembered but had not revisited for a long time. The deep full blue light glanced about and moved with the waves on the walls of the cave; her hands and arms were bathed in the light, and Akil himself, large and strong on the prow of the boat, looked like a statue cast in clay and then painted deep blue.

"It is so wondrously beautiful," murmured Atlanta.

"But we mustn't look at the light. We must search for the hidden currents of the water. Let us put down our measurers." She unrolled a long, weighted cord, and, as Akil rowed her about, she quickly took soundings. Then she let another cord float on the surface to see which way the water moved it.

"There is no whirlpool here," she said, "but there is a strange suction from the back of the cave. Are you sure there is not an opening underneath? How much time do we have?"

"A short time now."

"Hold the boat."

Atlanta stood in the boat, slipped out of her light pleated robe to the woven body cover she wore for swimming, and dived into the deepest part of the water. It was some time before she came up again.

"Hurry now. Tell me later," ordered Akil, and he hauled her safely aboard and pushed off toward the narrowing opening of the cave, with one strong movement.

Atlanta sat panting and pressed back her dripping hair.

"Down below, a long way below—twice your height, Akil—there is an opening where the sea water seeps in. If we could close it somehow, then we could enlarge the opening of the cave as well, and it would be safe."

They were out in the sunlight again, moving on the shining waters of the cove.

"But doing that might change the color," he said thoughtfully. "Should we do that?"

"I must think," murmured Atlanta. "Perhaps not. But

did you notice that the roof of the cave is very high? We might make a kind of—a kind of refuge of it."

"A refuge?"

"We might need such a refuge some day," she said. And she thought sadly of Baka. Baka did not feel an affinity with the sea, and he was neither a good swimmer nor an oarsman. A refuge somewhere in the sea would be safe from Baka.

She sighed. Poor Baka.

5

ON other days, when everything was propitious, they visited the other caves—the one of the violet light, and the one with the green glow.

On the day they went into the Violet Cave, Akil had a bandage on his arm. The day before, he had cut his arm while repairing the mill. One of the rocks that lined the canals had fallen against him, its jagged edge bruising and tearing his flesh, and he saw with annoyance that infection was beginning there. The arm was swollen and had turned an angry red around the wound.

Aurora had begged to be allowed to accompany them this time, and Akil had calculated the tides to the moment. Both girls wore their woven bathing dresses under their short pleated robes and had their hair bound back.

"First, let me bind your hurt arm," said Atlanta.

Akil shook off the kind hand, but not roughly. "Afterward, Sister," he said. "It hurts a little, but it's just a trifle. I can row strongly. And this is the very moment when we must push off."

Without discussion, the girls jumped into the boat and Akil started it skimming over the water. Akil had resources of power in his big body that seemed inexhaustible, for Atlanta, touching his arm, felt the fever in it, the hot pumping of the blood, and she knew that his head ached. But she also knew that he did not like to be ordered about by women, and so she was silent, determined to make her studies of the Violet Cave as quickly as possible and get back with Akil to where she would be allowed to tend him.

This time the hour was early in the morning. The sun had not been up more than a short time, and its rays still slanted over the earth, making all the dewdrops sparkle like jewels. There were a few thick white clouds in the sky and they seemed to come racing toward them.

The Violet Cave was beyond the Blue Cave, and it was much larger, though the light inside was fitful and there were days when it showed only the palest lavender. The Blue Cave was always drenched with the rich deep color of its light.

The opening through which they entered the cave was wider but shallower. Even at this propitious moment, all three had to bend down and keep their heads low. Once inside, though, both girls gasped with pleasure. For this was one of the good moments. The violet of the color in the cave seemed to be a living thing, leaping and moving about, touching everything with a sheen of soft color that was a shade between rose and blue and partook of each.

Atlanta reeled out her weighted measurer. Here the floor of the cave was not so deep, and when she spun out her markers on the surface, the water seemed to be docile enough.

"I doubt if there is any opening below," she said. "But I'll look."

She was not down long, and when she emerged and clambered into the boat, her face was radiant.

"No openings below. I felt all about. And look how high the walls are, up above. We could build shelves into them, which would never be touched by the tide."

"Hard work, and dangerous, waiting for the tides," murmured Akil.

"But we can manage!" she cried gleefully. "We will manage."

"What are you talking about, Atlanta?" asked Aurora.

Akil had propelled them toward the cave opening. A rising wave almost closed the aperture, so he waited, and then, at the exact moment when the wave subsided, he swung them swiftly through.

"I will tell you when we get back to the house. Akil, come with me to my room and I will dress your arm. Did you get it wet?"

"A little. It feels better, though."

"Well, sea water cannot hurt. And I will freshen the bandage and bind on some healing leaves."

They beached the boat and walked back to the house in good humor. Aurora ran ahead to get them all beakers of milk heated and sweetened with honey, and Akil also ate a barley cake. The girls shook out and dried their hair, and then Atlanta said, "I'll see to your arm now, Akil. And thank you for this morning."

When she unwound the bandage he was wearing, she paled. For his arm was smooth, unmarred by bruise or wound. She looked up at him in wonder.

"Strange," he murmured. "I feel different too. My headache is gone."

"And the long briar scratch on my leg, which was deep and just scabbing over," added Aurora, "has disappeared."

"There is some healing power in that violet light," said Atlanta slowly. "Which were the children who went into the Violet Cave? Let us go to see their parents and find out if any of the children had the same experience."

"Mother will remember which children visited the caves," said Aurora. "Let us talk to her."

Mara was busy in her weaving room, where she liked to work in the early hours of the day; she went later to the fields or to the processing rooms of the saffron, to oversee the work being done. She was treadling the pedals and casting the shuttles that threw the thread swiftly, weaving a subtle design in the gossamer-thin stuff. It was the soft, clinging, hand-woven material of which she made her own robes and those of her daughters.

The material she was weaving this time was of a delicate shade of rose, and she looked up from her loom smiling as her daughters entered the room. Flowers in a vase were sending out a gentle perfume, which was wafted around the room by the breeze coming in through the open window.

"Mother," Atlanta, Akil, and Aurora began all at once.

"What is it? What has happened?"

The three told her, all together, breathlessly.

Mara laid a hand on her heart. "It is miraculous," she whispered. "It is like what we were told as children about the ancient peoples who cured with light and vibrations from different tones struck upon a stone, or wood, or crystal. By all means, find the mothers of the children who went into the Violet Cave and learn what they have to tell you."

The story was the same at each cottage, and at first the Archers were elated. Then they became very serious as they realized the significance of what they were hearing. One mother said her child had had a broken arm when small, which had been badly set and swung in a strange position from his body. Now it was firm and true and could be used easily; one would never know it had been broken.

One child had been coughing, with the beginning of a chest congestion, which had cleared immediately. The mother had noticed and rejoiced, but she hadn't looked for the reason. There were stories of scratches and bruises that had inexplicably disappeared. Most impressive was the report of one of the women who worked in the drying rooms. Aurora knew her well; Shanna had married rather late in life and had had only one child, a little girl who was strong and straight in her limbs but unaccountably slow mentally. Little Shanni, as the child was called, had gone into the Violet Cave.

"And this morning she spoke clearly to me," marveled the mother, with tears of joy in her eyes, "and she asked me to teach her to read. I have tried to do it countless times but she never could remember the symbols for the sounds and she always said it gave her a headache. But today she learned quickly and began to sound the words! Aurora, what is it? What has happened?"

"We have discovered a wonderful thing, Shanna," said Atlanta, "but we cannot tell it to everyone yet, for people might become excited and rush into the Violet Cave when it is not safe. The light in that cave has some divine property which cures. We are certain of it now. Do not tell anyone until we have done what we can to establish times when the cave should be visited, have appointed guardians, and so on. But you will hear this from us as soon as anyone else! And, meanwhile, let me know exactly how long this magical help seems to last for little Shanni. And we are so happy, so happy for you!"

The three walked solemnly back to their home. Drako was waiting for them on the veranda.

"Your mother has told me about the light in the Violet Cave," he said. "I have been there as a boy, and so have others. But I suppose we never noticed any healing powers—perhaps we were not in need of them then. Or perhaps we were just unobservant. I don't know. But sit down, children. I have remembered something my grandfather told me, and now you should know it."

The three sat down, and Drako marshaled his thoughts. "I was a small boy when he told me these things I am about to tell you. He had been told them by his grandfather. They were prophecies, warnings of something to come."

Drako paused and looked into each young face. Atlanta's lovely features were composed, but her expression was remote and thoughtful. Aurora's face still radiated the happiness she had felt for Shanna and little Shanni. Akil looked oppressed. The news had upset him, for he was a very simple soul, and magical things awakened in him a kind of awe akin to fear.

"As you children know, my family has worked these lands and has raised and dried and packed the sacred flower for many generations. It must be about five or six generations back—you can count out what ancestor-grandfather it must have been—when one of our family (and we were always called the Archers) was visited by an angel of prophecy.

"It was almost sundown—so it was told to me—and the sea was smooth and quiet, just whispering against the sand, and our ancestor, then a young man, had gone for a walk. He was a good young man, they all say, and truthful, but there were some in the family who did not believe him when he came back and said he had spoken with a heavenly being who had told him a secret of the future.

"The angel, he said, was enormous, filling almost all the sky, with great wings that reached from one horizon to the other, and his whole being was colored with the glow of the setting sun—rose and pink and gold and palest green. The angel spoke to him by name, and his name was the same as mine: Drako.

" 'Drako,' said the angel, 'listen to me, and ponder my words, for I have been sent by the Supreme Spirit to give you a warning!'

"My ancestor, that Drako, was terrified, he told his family, but at the same time he felt respect, even love, for the great creature that filled the sky.

"It was told that the angel was enormous and at the same time his voice was intimate and kind; and the angel was transparent, for the clouds and the outline of the hills and everything around shone through him. But then the vision seemed to draw himself together, to pull all his component parts inward somehow, and become smaller and smaller, until he stood in front of Drako as a young man with curling brown hair and eyes as blue as the sea. He had wings, but as he became smaller he closed them, and they covered his back with an iridescent white cloak.

"That Drako of long ago answered, 'Tell me. I listen.'

" 'Listen and obey,' said the angel. 'Give me your promise.'

" 'I promise,' said Drako.

" 'Atlantis has been dear to the heart of Our Master, the Supreme One. He has guided Atlanteans to settle and colonize other lands and take them knowledge and skills and science. He has elevated Atlantean heroes and made them into gods who are worshipped in the far places, as Poseidon, Hercules, and Zeus are worshipped.

He has protected Atlantis and sent her great gifts. But the Supreme Spirit and every creature to which he has given life must be respected.

" 'There will come a time, Drako, and your descendants will see it, when wisdom will give way to greed, and generosity to love of power. When this happens, the Supreme Spirit has sworn to sink Atlantis beneath the waves, forever and ever.'

"My ancestor Drako told that when he heard those words 'Forever and ever' they sounded like the drums of death which are played at funerals. And they became mixed with other sounds in his ears—a terrible roaring and rushing and grinding and growling, as if the bowels of the earth were to open and swallow everything in sight. Drako grew dizzy at this and almost fainted, but the angel put out a hand and touched him, and strength flowed from the hand and filled Drako with valor.

" 'There will be signs,' the angel said, 'so that you may be on your guard. There will be a sign in the water, that you or your descendants may read, which will tell you that the time for testing is near. There will be a sign in the sky, afterward, which is a further warning. And a special sign of grace from the Supreme Spirit will be sent to one of you, your own family, your own descendants, to use for good or ill. You will know when that sign has been made manifest.'

"And then, Drako my ancestor said, then the angel again became large and larger and he spread his wings and filled the whole sky, and then he disappeared and the sky was left clear and deep blue with nothing to show at all but a thin sickle moon and one star.

"Drako my ancestor then fell on the sand and prayed, and wept, and swayed back and forth. He had been through a terrible experience, something awe-inspiring, and he did not know how to tell about it. Also, he was afraid no one would believe him. But he himself believed. He said that nothing in his life had ever been more real, more wondrous, than the angel who spoke to him.

"He gathered his family around—but he was not the oldest brother, not even the second oldest, and so they did not accord him great authority. When he spoke, some listened. Others laughed. But all remembered. And every now and then they spoke, among themselves only —for it seemed to be a family thing, and they never told it outside the family circle—about what the signs might be and when they would appear.

"My own grandfather told me the story, and I have thought about it sometimes. But it seems to me now that one of the signs may have come to us. The special grace."

He paused and looked at his children.

"The special grace?" Atlanta said. "No. The Violet Cave is a treasure for us all to guard. But the special grace is to come to one person. Only one, to use for good or ill."

"And the other signs, Father?" Aurora asked fearfully.

"I have not seen anything," Drako said. "But we must keep watch, my children."

He dropped his head and was deep in thought for some time. Then he turned before going into the house, and said, "You must tell no one of these things. They are not to be known outside of the family."

All three laid their hands on their hearts in agreement and promise.

6

AS the days went by, Akil worked whenever he could at stopping the water seepage in the Blue Cave and turning it into a haven. At first he seemed to make no progress, so short were the moments when he could be inside the cave, but he was faithful and never missed a chance to go in, bringing tools for boring holes in the rock sides of the cave. Eventually he took wood to thrust into the holes into which he could set hooks. Finally he had all the hooks into the cave walls and he was proud of his accomplishment. He told Aurora and Atlanta of his plan to have many hammocks woven, to swing from the hooks, well above the water, where people could be hidden; supplies of food and water could be taken in and swung from the highest hammocks. Thus the cave would be a safe and secret refuge, should it be needed some day.

The girls wove the hammocks. They went to the foothills not far from their home and there gathered plants which yielded a strong fiber, and this they wove into firm thin cords, wetting them with sea water to make them both elastic and strong. Aram had shown them how this was done, for all sorts and sizes of cords were used in the making of boats. No metal was ever introduced into the wood, for nails or screws made of metal would wrench the wood apart. The planks of the boats were fitted and bound together in such a way as to conserve their flexibility in high or rough seas.

Among the families who lived on Archer land and worked among the sacred lilies of the saffron were several girls who were friends of Aurora and Atlanta. They often accompanied the twins on their excursions to gather fiber plants and helped in the making of the cords, though of course they did not know the reason for this activity. They made of the sessions times of joy and picnicking, and later on several of the girls helped Atlanta and Aurora to knot the hammocks.

One jolly dark-haired girl, with a smattering of freckles across her tilted nose, and long amber eyes shaded by black lashes, thought she had discovered the reason for the activity. "One of you is preparing for her marriage!" she said.

This friend, whose name was Vega, was often chosen by Akil for the dancing and as his partner in the running games, for she was swift and strong. Vega was playful;

she tossed her mane of black hair and teased Akil and flirted with him. He never knew whether she preferred him to other young men or thought him a great bore, and so he was rather shy with her and could not think of any words when he was with her.

Atlanta looked up from knotting the strong cords. "Oh, Vega, you will marry before either of us!" she said, and Vega hung her head and turned dark red.

"I have been asked in marriage," she confided. But she did not look excited or happy.

"And what do your parents say?"

"They will not urge me," she said, but Aurora saw the glint of tears in the amber eyes.

"Don't accept anyone who does not please you," cried Aurora, pausing in her tying of cords. The girls had tinted the cords in different shades, so as to guide them in making hammocks of different sizes—white for children, green for women, and brown for men.

Vega had swift and skillful fingers in the knotting, too, and was a valued help. She paused and her hands were idle.

"The man who has asked for me is good and hardworking and does no evil," she said. "He is a merchant from the town who sells supplies to the mariners. He is a widower with four children and has a good house, and he would be good to me."

"He will find another wife," said Atlanta. "A widow with little ones of her own, who will be grateful for a home and will wait on him and be very happy. You must marry Akil, who loves you."

Vega put down her work and leaped up and ran from the room where the girls were working.

"Now you have spoiled things," complained Aurora. "You have frightened her."

"On the contrary," laughed Atlanta. "Now she will be shy and quiet, and poor Akil will be encouraged to speak. You will see."

"Anyhow, we have lost a helper," murmured Aurora.

"She'll be back."

And Atlanta was right. Before sundown Vega slipped in once more and took up some cords and began knotting them very busily in the hammock design.

When the light failed and the girls began to gather up their work to put it away, Akil appeared in the doorway, looking, as always, tremendously large and strong and dark.

"I have come," he said, "to ask who would like to walk along the beach with me. The hour is beautifully calm and the sea is soft, soft as satin along the sand."

"Why, I would like to walk with you," answered Vega, and she rose and went to stand by his side. They went out and started toward the cove, and as they walked, they held hands and swung them in rhythm.

Atlanta laughed joyously as she picked up the cords and knotting hooks that had fallen from Vega's lap when she rose.

"We must tell her about the caves, the magic light, and everything," said Aurora, catching Atlanta's thought.

"Yes," said Atlanta. "But I am glad about this. For she is a good person, and strong. And you know I must be leaving. I must go so very soon now. I want you to have someone by your side to talk with, to help you, to be close."

Aurora put her head down on her arms and burst into tears. "Why can't I go with you?" she mourned as she had done every month or two for years, ever since she knew that Atlanta was to be a Sea Priestess.

"You cannot because you must be here, watchful and ready to look after our parents and all the people here," said Atlanta solemnly. "I will send you thoughts and I will keep you close in my prayers. You will see, you will have my presence with you even more than now, for I will need you to keep your mind open toward me, ready to listen, to accept my messages."

"Atlanta, you see bad times ahead, trouble."

"I am afraid. But maybe, maybe we will be spared. It will depend on many things—perhaps even on one person."

"Baka," said Aurora, reading Atlanta's thought instantly.

"Baka," whispered Atlanta.

7

T H E day dawned when Atlanta was to be received into the Sisterhood of the Sea Priestesses at Hesperidia. The ceremony was to take place in the afternoon, at the moment of the turning of the tide toward the shore, so Atlanta spent part of the morning visiting all her favorite spots and saying goodbye to her friends.

There were smiles, but also tears, as they embraced her and wished her well and asked her to pray for them. Old men who worked in the fields transplanting the bulbs of the saffron, young men who fired the ovens for drying the pistils, women who had worked with her in the plucking and the drying rooms, and playmates of her childhood, all were both glad and sorry to see her go.

Drako had named responsible persons to watch over

the fields and the processing rooms while they were gone, for the whole family and many other families from the estate were going to watch the ceremony. Aram was coming for them in his first boat, now that he proudly wore the trident on his shoulder. It was not long after dawn that they saw his white sails shining against the blue of the sea as he rounded the point and came into the calm cove. There he dropped anchor and let down a small boat to bring his passengers out to the larger vessel, which lay rocking gently on the water.

All the family and friends were wearing their best clothes, all but Atlanta, who wore an old soft pleated gown of palest fog gray which had been washed many times. Her gown for the ceremony was wrapped and ready in a bundle. She was to take nothing from her home, save her ritual gown, the priestesses had told Mara. It was to be a complete break with her old home and the old life, for the priestesses never left their temple to return home, though they could occasionally receive visits from relatives or close friends.

Aurora could not help enjoying the trip around the point, along the shore, and into the great bay of Hesperidia, despite the sad errand. The prospect of parting from Atlanta was so painful to her that she tried not to think of it at all, and only her own best gown, of changeable gauze, which showed now rose, now gold, recalled to her that her twin was to be taken from her forever.

Aram stood in the prow of his boat and kept it on course, signaling to his two helpers—apprentices, as he had been an apprentice for some years—how to manage the sails. There was music on board, and the young people danced; a stiff breeze kept the sails well out and sent them skimming over the waves.

Atlanta sat in the prow, near her brother. In the years to come he would be nearest to her, for he too served the sea, the Great Ocean, which was to be her god. Often he turned to smile at her, and she smiled back. She had made her farewells, in person and in her mind and heart, for some time past. Now she was ready, looking forward with great joy to her initiation.

When Aram's vessel drew into the bay and Aram ordered the sails furled, he brought them up close beside a dock which was built out into the bay, alongside the entrance of the Great Canal, where the closed gates showed that the tide was going out at the other end. As Atlanta stepped ashore, two priestesses came forward, each taking one of her hands.

Thus they approached Mara and Drako and bowed deeply to them. "We thank you for the gift of your daughter to the Great Ocean," they said solemnly in unison.

Drako rose and answered, in words that were customary. "We surrender our child to the Great Ocean, and to you, the Priestesses of the Sea, with hearts full of devotion."

Atlanta embraced her father and mother, but gently, as if her mind were already far away, far out in the deep waters, where she would presently go to take part in the ritual. And then they went away in a small boat on the canal. From where the family and friends stood on the dock, they could see the round stone towers of the temple she would enter.

"Well," said Drako, drawing a long sigh, "let us go now to the other side so that we can see them when they come down to the bay and put out to sea."

Mara also sighed deeply, but then she smiled and said, "Let us have more music, please, musicians! Flutes and drums! This is a joyous occasion."

Mara was recalling that only one girl in several hundred was chosen by the priestesses even though many parents, in gestures of zeal, offered their daughters. The priestesses had to be perfect in health and appearance, and intelligent, good, and gifted in the ancient Atlantean mystery of reading and sending thoughts. In the latter days there were few who still retained this gift, and they could not explain how or why they knew they had it or in what way they used it.

Accompanied by their musicians, and strolling along the beach front of the town, the party moved toward the other opening of the canal, located near the docks of Aram's school. He had arranged for the family and friends to occupy benches, spread with bright covers and shaded by awnings, in the best place, with a view of the canal, the bay, and the sea beyond. Aram's teachers waited there to welcome the Archers, and servants passed among them with refreshing drinks, honey cakes, and other delicacies.

Soon they saw the festive vessel of the Sea Priestesses

coming down the canal, for the tide was going out swiftly to sea and would carry their bark out to the wide expanse of water where they performed their rites.

The priestesses all wore light silken gowns of sea blue and sea green, with shells beaded on long cords to tie about their waists, and crowns of shells, which flashed iridescent colors in the sunlight. Their hair flowed free; their arms and legs and feet were bare. Among them they saw Atlanta, still wearing her old gray dress.

The barge passed the Archers, who stood and cheered; and a crowd which had gathered round for the ceremonies joined them in shouts and singing. Atlanta did not look up; her eyes were fixed on the horizon, where the sea seemed to be softly breathing, the waves rising and falling in steady rhythm.

Baka had arrived late. He saluted his parents and his brothers and Aurora, and then took his place close to his sister. He was wearing his dark brown student dress, as usual, but on his brow was a mark in red dye—a circle surrounding a star.

"Oh, Baka!" cried Aurora, noticing it. "Have you been given some honor?"

"Yes, I have. But I can't tell about it. Later, perhaps." He couldn't keep himself from adding, "It is rather more wonderful than anything you can suppose!"

"More wonderful than Atlanta's reception today?"

"Much more."

"That is hard to believe."

"Well, I advise you to believe it," he answered, annoyed, and went to sit beside Aram, whom he had always secretly admired and loved, even while resenting his position as oldest brother.

"Do you have a glass, Aram, to make them large, so that we can see everything out there?" asked Baka.

"Yes, I have a seaman's glass."

"I have one of ours. They loaned it to me for today. It is better than yours. Stronger."

"Then let Mother and Aurora use it," said Aram with equanimity.

Baka approached his mother and offered her his long glass. She thanked him and set it to her eye.

"Oh, how extraordinary!" she cried with pleasure. "This glass has brought the whole barge so close to me! They are undressing Atlanta now. They are going to put her into the sea!"

Baka was immediately sorry he did not have the glass himself; he would have liked to see the priestesses toss Atlanta into the deep.

"She has gone down," whispered Mara, not taking the long magnifying glass from her eye. "She has gone deep. She hasn't come up yet." Mara's voice shook with anxiety.

"Atlanta told me," comforted Aurora, "that initiates tried to stay down, far down, as long as possible, to hear what the Sea God, the Great Ocean, would tell them. All the initiates do it."

"Oh, I wish she would come up," cried Mara. "Oh, it worries me!"

Drako gently took the glass from her. "Let me look," he said, and carefully set the glass against his eye, rising to get a full sweeping view. With an exclamation, he quickly handed the glass back to his wife. "She has come up," he said. "They are taking her into the boat again."

Mara seized the glass. Baka moved quickly from Aram, who was sharing his glass with Aurora, to his parents. He began to feel angry. It was *his* glass, and nobody was allowing him to use it.

"They have taken her into the prow and they are dressing her in a green-and-blue robe like the others! Now they are giving her a girdle of shells. And—"

"Let me see, please," put in Baka, and his mother released the glass to him with a grateful smile.

Baka saw his sister being crowned with a diadem of shells that had been polished to shining pearl.

"Now they will come back," he said, losing interest, and he passed the glass to Akil. Akil instantly let Vega have it.

Within a half hour the barge came into view again, and if Atlanta had not still been in the prow with the high priestess, Selene, they would have had trouble finding her among the others, for now all were alike. Only the long hair, streaming in the breeze, was of varied colors—reddish brown, dark brown, black, coppery, and the shining gold of Atlanta's.

The barge went toward the farther gate of the canal, now open, and passed from sight.

"I am ready to sail you home again," said Aram.

"We have time to walk home before dark," sighed Drako, who suddenly felt very sad. "Who would like to walk home with me?"

The family and all the visitors agreed at once to walk. They were thoughtful and supposed that Aram might have other duties to attend to early in the morning and they hesitated to take his time.

So farewells were said. "Will you come home with us, Baka?" asked his mother. "Could you get permission?"

"No. I must go back," he said.

He could have asked and received permission, but the first of the new experiments was to take place in the early morning and he did not wish to miss any of it.

Bowing to his parents and his older brothers and the guests, he turned and strode off toward the city.

8

THAT night, when darkness came down and the stars began to shine in the black sky, Aurora sat in the room she had shared with Atlanta. By the light of a small lamp which burned continually because of some imprisoned energy and which had to be capped with a dark cover to extinguish its light, she sorted out and folded away the things that Atlanta had left behind. Her dresses—biege and rose and pale green and pale yellow; woven bands for the hair; laces for her sandals. There were even two pairs of sandals, one very much worn and almost showing the imprint of Atlanta's slender foot. Aurora wrapped these in a soft cloth and put them away for a keepsake. The others, scarcely worn, she would use herself. In a chest which the two girls had shared were Atlanta's adornments: two bracelets of gold, one with a shining blue stone; a diadem of white metal, with a pearl centered in it just above the brow; a woven cloak of white wool, to wear when the winds were cold; and a girdle made of silver links. In the chest were her scarves; a folding book into which she wrote with a sharp instrument that shed its own ink along the letters as she wrote; sets of bandages and medicines, for Atlanta knew how to care for many kinds of injuries; her small collection of stones and shells and pressed flowers; and her vials of homemade perfume.

Aurora capped her light and went to sit by the window. Usually she did not hear the sea unless she was listening for it; she lived with its sound beating against her, day and night, as with the sound of her own heart.

But on this night she listened intently, to try to hear what the sea might tell her. But though the waves rushed into the cove, broke hissing on the sands, and whispered away as always, they did not speak to her heart. Turning her eyes upward toward the stars, she consciously emptied her mind of everything and waited for a thought to come—and suddenly she heard Atlanta's voice.

"Sleep well, dear sister. And prepare a welcome, for Set is coming toward you over the water. Sleep well."

Aurora sat on longer, but she was comforted and after a time, when her favorite bright star had wheeled above and out of sight behind the house, she lay down and slept instantly.

In the Temple of the Sea Priestesses, Atlanta had been shown her room. It was very small, a tiny stone cubicle with a narrow slit of window. There was little furniture in it: a small chest, and a cot that let down from the wall and could be pushed back up into place, out of the way, when the occupant of the cell was not sleeping. There was one cushioned, wool-covered bench, and a leaf that let down from the wall in the same manner as the cot, serving as a writing table. It held a writing instrument and many leaves of cloth-like fiber.

There was no lamp. "You will not need one," said Selene, "for there is always light in the hall, and there are no doors to our rooms. Our privacy, when we need it, is in our minds. Very often we pray most of the night—especially when we know the Great Ocean is angry and ready to devour ships and men and lash against the towns on the coast. We have kept the Great Ocean calm and happy for many moons, but we have had messages that he has been enraged by winds and lightnings toward the east and his anger is rising. Tonight we will all pray. Only you, because you have come to us today, are to sleep now. I will call you in the morning."

"In your prayers, good Mother, ask for the safety of an Egyptian mariner, Set, who is on the high seas, please. He is to be the husband of my sister."

"We will pray for him."

And Selene, the Mother Priestess, glided away.

Atlanta at once let down her cot and lay down upon it,

her arms crossed upon her bosom. In her mind she returned to the dark cool depths into which she had entered, naked, when she was consecrated to the sea. She recalled the coolness, then the cold, of the water, which darkened as she fell swiftly downward. She did not reach the bottom, but she saw and then felt sea creatures passing her, knew that her hair was streaming upward. She had kept her eyes open, for she had thought she might see some wondrous thing. When at last her lungs felt as if they might burst, she kicked and propelled herself upward, and kicked and kicked again, to reach the surface and the light.

Had the Great Ocean spoken to her, they had asked her after they had dried her and helped her catch her breath and after they had given her a drink of some warming liquid that made her body tingle with life again.

"He spoke," answered Atlanta, in great wonder. "He spoke into my innermost ear, and I heard his words."

"What were they?" asked the Mother Priestess.

"I heard these words said: 'Child, obey me. Listen and obey.' That is all I was told."

Selene had smiled.

"It was an important message," she said to Atlanta. "We will teach you to be even more alert for the Great Ocean's voice; you will hear it inside your ear, deep inside, as inside a shell, counseling you, and you must tell us what you hear, so that we may all be prepared."

"You know, then, what will happen to us all?" Atlanta asked.

"We know, just as you have always known. Only we do not know the day or the hour."

Atlanta felt the sea swinging her cot softly, she felt little fishes and strands of sea plants caress her body, and she slipped into slumber as into the deep still water.

9

BY the next day the first edges of the storm had reached Poseida. The waves awakened Aurora before it was light. She heard the roaring and crashing of the great breakers as they washed through the arches and pounded on the shore, and the shrieking of the wind. Sea birds, flying inland, gave harsh, worried cries. The cattle were lowing in the fields. Aurora leaped up, suddenly wide-awake, and threw on her dress and a shawl.

Her parents were already up and outside, for the wind was harsh and cold and might harm the new saffron plants just coming up out of the earth.

As her eyes became accustomed to the darkness, and as it began to grow lighter, Aurora saw that everyone who lived and worked at the Arches was out in the fields, covering the plants with gauze and anchoring the gauze to the earth with two edged spikes. Even so, the wind tugged at the gauze, unwilling to be foiled. Aurora, too, gathered up gauze and spikes and ran to where she seemed to be needed and there began to work as swiftly and efficiently as she could. The wind rose to more and more furious wails and gusts, and twice she was knocked down into the flowers, almost suffocating from the heavy sweet smell.

Ramo, working nearby, called to her, though the wind seized the words from his mouth and blew them away as soon as he had formed them.

"If we save the newest growth, that will be something," he tried to call to her. "I think the older plants, being taller, will surely be pulled up."

They worked all day, only stopping to rest when they could not move any more. The winds began to abate toward midafternoon and a rain fell. There were large warm drops at first and then a steady, cold downpour.

When the rain began, Drako gave the signal for everyone to go in.

"We can do no more," he said. "We must let the Storm Gods take the rest, as they will."

The people, bedraggled, mud-covered, and wringing wet, staggered back toward the buildings, and women started fires at once and began to heat milk and honey and various leaf teas and to bring out loaves, which they heated through. Squares of salty cheese were distributed. At first the people were almost too exhausted to eat, but the steaming teas warmed them and they began to eat and to talk.

"There hasn't been a storm like this in my lifetime," said one elderly man who was sitting near Drako. "My father and grandfather told me of such storms," he said, "but we have never had anything so furious in my life. I wonder how they have fared in Hesperidia."

"And on the sea," murmured Aurora, who was thinking of Set. She added, "I hope our Aram was not out on the water."

Akil went out to stare around him, heedless of the rain, which still fell, and the wind, which still swirled about. "I think it is abating now," he said, shielding his eyes with his hand. "Come, Aurora, I will help you home so that you can change into dry clothes."

Aurora went out, the rain chilling her again at once, but supported by Akil's strength they made their way against the wind from the sea and were able to reach the veranda of their house.

As they went into the great hall of the house, Aurora stood quite still for a moment, an expression of listening and of attention on her face.

"I thought," she said to Akil, "I thought Atlanta was sending me a message. So strange. She said—I think she said, 'This is a prophecy. Tell everyone.' "

"A prophecy? But then she didn't go on, she didn't say what the prophecy was?"

"No. Just 'This is a prophecy.' Akil, she must mean the storm. And if it is a prophecy, we will have another storm like this. Worse, even."

"There have been prophecies like that always," he said, his big faithful face wrinkled into a look of consternation.

"Well . . . perhaps I misunderstood. I am not as clever, or as spiritual, as Atlanta. She will speak to me again, I hope." Aurora was almost fainting with weariness, and Akil picked her up as easily as if she were a sack of barley and slung her over his shoulder. He strode with her down the hall to her room and laid her on her bed. He covered her and then left.

He was worried about the caves and all the work he had done upon them with such effort. Perhaps the pegs for hammocks were all loosened or pulled out; perhaps the wooden blocks he had set into the stone walls to hold the hooks were damaged. Perhaps—and the thought hurt him, for its implications—perhaps the entrances had been blocked by other stones, or changed in some way. He struggled down toward the shore of the cove, against the wind and the waves, to look toward the distant point where the caves, and the arches that gave their land its name, should show. But the sea was too high and the rain too heavy. He could scarcely make out the arches, and he could not see the farther caves at all.

10

BAKA sat in his cell in the science laboratory and watched the storm exultantly. Just that one moment, he thought, and the crystal hasn't even begun to accumulate all its power yet!

He was a trusted worker in the laboratory where the new invention had been thought out and calculated and where the production of a peculiarly powerful crystal was slowly taking place. The crystal was of a substance that absorbed and held power in abeyance for future use. Once the maximum power had been absorbed by the crystal, it would give off rays that could destroy all life. Lakon did not mean to use it for such purposes; he hoped to focus the rays on the moon and distant stars and learn more about them. Scientists and students were busy in the laboratories at the same time perfecting telescopes and magnifying glasses.

Baka had been consumed with curiosity about the powers already in the crystal, and in a moment when he was left alone with it—with instructions to train certain intensified rays from the sun upon it—he had momentarily loosed one ray. Not having the apparatus to focus it, he had merely freed the crystal for an instant. For only a moment had he dared to reverse the action of the crystal from absorption to release—but it had thrilled him with a sense of power that shook him with emotion. To own this power! To use it himself, himself alone! It would make him master of the world.

Instantly he stifled the thought. He did not stifle it because he was ashamed but only because he feared some Atlantean who still had the ancient gifts of thought transference might catch his own excitement and interpret it, even betray him to the science master, Lakon.

Baka turned his eyes back to the raging sea and the tearing winds. Stones, torn from the walls by the winds, were flying over the city; the water in the canals was rushing from the sea and back in furious, white-tipped, curling waves; there was a roaring sound that drummed in the ears. The ray must have lacked strength as yet to reach out into space, thought Baka. It had probably described a curve and sent its power into the sea, causing this awe-inspiring storm.

To hide his thoughts, he sent his mind to the Arches and gave momentary interest to whether the family buildings had been able to withstand the storm. For a moment he started up in worry. Would the saffron flow-ers, the sacred crop, be destroyed? If so, it might affect his being able to stay on in the laboratory, since Drako paid the science masters a regular measure of the sacred flower pistils for Baka's education.

I must be careful, thought Baka. So careful. And I must keep my secret. No one must ever know.

He resolved not to touch the Power Stone again, no matter what his opportunity, until he had perfected a complete plan, until he was ready to act.

11

WHEN at last the storm had spent itself, Drako, Ramo, and Akil inspected their fields and buildings to take note of the losses. About a third of the crop was badly damaged.

"We will have to replant," sighed Drako.

"We should gather all the flowers that were blown down," Akil said, "and take the pistils and dry them most carefully. They are water-soaked and mired, but we can save a portion."

The buildings where the plucking and drying and packing was done had been blown in, but the ovens were still well-anchored and in order.

"We can start building new sheds at once. It won't take too long," said Ramo. "I'll organize a team to go out to the hills to cut the lumber and gather the building stones. I believe we can have things in order in ten days —perhaps a few days over ten."

"The house was not badly damaged. Nor the homes of the workers," reported Akil. "Being built of stone and well-mortared and close to earth, they resisted the wind. The waters from the sea boiled into the cove and up on the land some distance, but the waves did not come anywhere near as far inland as they did on the unprotected sea side."

"I wonder about the Caves of Light," murmured Akil. "I cannot think of trying to go in for several days more. The sea is still too high."

So the Archers were busy repairing the damage done. In the fields there was great activity to salvage all that could be taken up; and where mud and sea water had washed over too much of the planting, the fields were to be plowed again and prepared for new sowing.

Aurora and her mother worked busily with swift fingers, extracting the pistils from damaged flowers.

"These bricks of saffron must be clearly marked 'damaged,' " instructed Mara.

Aurora's thoughts were almost continuously on Set since the storm. Atlanta had sent a thought that he was on the Great Ocean, but there had been no message since from her twin. Aurora took comfort in this, for she believed that if Set had come to harm, Atlanta would have known and sent her the news.

Set was indeed on his way to Poseida, but with a badly damaged vessel. He and his men were busy bailing night and day, for the ship took water badly and there was no way to patch it. They were still miles from harbor, but Set kept the spirits of his men up. He started them singing, and he rationed out some of the sweets Atlanta had made for him and presented as a gift. The candy, so succulently sweet and crunchy with nuts and seeds, gave the men new energy. As soon as the wind was manageable, Set devised a sail by which he could direct his vessel. The main mast had gone down in the furious wind of the storm.

He was so busy trying to keep his men optimistic and his vessel afloat and moving that he had little time to try to send thoughts anywhere, though Aurora had shyly tried to teach him something of the method Atlanta had taught her.

"I fear I may never be more than a receiver," he had said humbly.

On that afternoon, some moons before, Aurora had turned to him with open affection. Set thought of these things as he went about the business of bringing his boat safely in. He had had to jettison a good part of his cargo during the fierce storm. Now the problem was to save his men and the vessel.

Set saw in his mind's eye, like a bright vision, the lovely face of the young girl, the very face of the one he had loved at once: Atlanta. And yet not the same. Aurora was more human, less strong in gifts and thoughts and ways that set Atlanta apart and made her a sort of priestess even before she entered the Temple of the Sea Priestesses.

Set had prayed to Atlanta during the night of the raging storm and darkness, and he believed that she had interceded with the Great Ocean Spirit to keep him and his men alive.

Yes, Atlanta was surrounded by a sort of aura which gave her beauty an unearthly glow. But Aurora, her mirror image, was warmer and closer. He could love Atlanta forever and never touch her, thought Set with awe, but whenever he was near Aurora he wanted to pass his hand over her golden hair, feel the warm curve of her soft cheek, touch her tender lips.

The sail opened and took the wind, and the damaged craft began to sail swiftly forward under Set's strong guiding hand.

That afternoon Aurora had said to him, "If you want to send a thought, you must first concentrate strongly and let everything you feel and see and smell and hear fall away from you, leaving you in a kind of semidetached state. Then you project your thought and you concentrate on it, sharpen it, tighten it, project it like a swift arrow through the distance to the one you wish to reach."

"Probably I will never be in a position to do this," he explained, "because I am a captain and my skill lies in keeping many things in my mind at once and forgetting nothing. There is so much furniture in the room of my mind all the time—I could not detach myself."

"Ah," said Aurora. "Perhaps one must lead a very simple life in order to acquire this power. Then surely Atlanta will become even more adept, for she has always been able to do it. I can project sometimes, but only when my emotion has already detached me from everything and made me think and feel nothing but the moment. But I am generally a good receiver."

"This is a curious art, here in Poseida. We do not know it in Egypt," Set said. "We go to our gods for information about the future and for guidance."

"Atlanta says the ancient peoples of Atlantis, who settled Poseida and even your Egypt countless centuries ago, all communicated in this way. They did not need to talk, although they did so for pleasure, in company. And they could communicate in poetry. They were a greatly advanced race. We have lost so many of their arts. Then once in a while there is a person like Atlanta who somehow has recaptured the spirit of those ancient people and, with their spirit, their gifts."

"She is most remarkable," he agreed.

"Atlanta tells me that the more scientific the mind and its activities, the more this receptivity to intuitions and ideas sent through the air by other people or by spirits is obscured," Aurora had said. "Perhaps you are of a scientific mind. Baka is like this. He can neither receive nor send thoughts. And neither can the masters he works with, though they are brilliant, the greatest minds we have in Poseida."

"I am not a scientist," Set said. "And I do have intuitions, moments when I feel the great spirits moving over the waters. Every sailor does. Perhaps I will be able to receive your thoughts sometimes, Aurora, if you will send them to me."

Her face broke into a radiant smile. "I will send you happy and affectionate thoughts every day," she promised.

But during the horrors of the storm, through the black night of lashing waves, with the pitching boat, and the crashing and creaking of masts and timbers, it was Atlanta to whom he had prayed.

12

B A K A went about his duties quietly and efficiently. He was almost never alone in the room with the Power Stone, as they all now called it. He set himself to pleasing his master and to learning everything he could about the possibilities of power in the crystal.

"But how will you begin to demonstrate the gifts of the crystal, after it has absorbed the maximum of concentrated power from the sun?" he asked Lakon when the student scientists had gathered in a classroom in the laboratory.

The master scientist laughed deprecatingly. "We are not obliged to make a diagram of that," he answered confidently. "We are master scientists, responsible to no one—not even to the Council. We simply work and think and do and invent. They will have to decide how to use the gifts of the Power Stone."

"But," Baka persisted, "there must be wonderful things this power could be used for—to help people."

He was skating on the edge of a thought. Baka wanted very much to know what sort of control might be exercised over the gifts of the crystal from outside the laboratory.

"We can think about all that later on," Lakon answered airily. "Right now we are attacking a mathematical problem. How fast will a beam from this crystal be returned to us if we bounce it off the moon, for example?"

But Baka still persisted. "Master, isn't it possible that the beam could penetrate and not bounce back from the moon? I mean, isn't it possible that it could *destroy* the moon?"

The master looked astounded for a moment and then he had his answer ready.

"Oh, we shall know that when we release our first power beam," he said. "Now the problem, students. And no more questions or speculations, please. We are scientists here—not interested in anything but *facts*. Remember that. Calculate the speed of the beam through space. Will it be the same speed as light? Concentrate now. I will leave you to your work."

Master Lakon wrapped his old, colorless gown around him and strode out of the room. By the way he walked, Baka knew he was annoyed. The master scientist had made many talks to the students advising them to keep their minds on observed and provable fact, and had constantly warned them about being diverted in their calculations by emotional speculation.

Baka was quick and clever with figures. But he was thinking about other things, too. I see, he said to himself, that I must begin to make friends. I cannot do what I plan alone. I must devise things to do and to say that will begin to draw people to me and make them loyal to me.

So he turned over in his mind a series of procedures. Would it be best to obligate people to himself, do them many favors and thus win them? He thought about this for some time. But, he decided, human nature is strange. Sometimes people do not like you if you do them too many favors. I have seen it happen that an injured or an old person turns on the one who would help him with an angry expression that says, as plain as words: Let me alone! On the other hand, if you permit someone to help you, Baka had observed, he will sometimes become your friend.

He decided on this last procedure, but in moderation. That would draw a few to him in the beginning, he realized, perhaps a sort of central core. A kind of high court. But he must have many followers, and followers are not loyal like friends, he realized. They will be deflected from your side by any show of weakness or by any reverses. I must think of some way to make them depend on me for something they can't get elsewhere, thought Baka.

He brooded over this problem many days but could find no solution within himself; therefore, one day, he asked for a holiday. The master scientist admired Baka's work, his clean figures, his accuracy, his general quietness, impersonality, and good behavior. He thought Baka would make an exemplary scientist; he even had it in mind to begin building him up as a possible master to teach in the laboratory. So permission was granted.

Baka bowed and thanked Lakon and gave as his excuse for requesting a holiday that he wanted to see how his family had fared during the great storm, about which people were still talking in Hesperidia.

On the day of his holiday Baka walked out into bright sunlight. He first went down to the docks, where Aram was now a captain. Luckily, he found his brother eating at one of the tables that were shared by captains and workers at the docks.

"May I join you?"

Aram looked up and saw his brother Baka bowing in the doorway. Baka had practiced making himself look mild and inoffensive, for he had seen that people were put off by his hostilities and he had decided to conquer and hide for the time being that streak of contentiousness in his nature.

"Greetings! Glad to see you," cried Aram. "Come and sit down."

Aram was broader and more darkly tanned than before. The tattooed trident on his shoulder stood out proudly; he wore a wide golden bracelet above the elbow, for he sometimes liked to train with the bull dancers in the country to keep himself in trim, for, as he said, the days at sea were exciting but sedentary. Bull dancers all wore this bracelet. Around Aram's long, almond-shaped brown eyes was a little fan of white wrinkles where the folded flesh had not tanned.

Aram piled Baka's plate with what all the men were eating: boiled vegetables with mushrooms and herbs, whole-grain bread, and cheese.

Baka ate slowly and daintily. He took from his pouch, which he wore suspended from the shoulders, a small packet wrapped in damp-proof paper, and sprinkled some powder on his food. "What is that?" asked Aram idly. "A kind of salt?"

"Yes. Exactly," said Baka. "Care to try it?"

Aram put a pinch on his vegetables, tasted, and made a face of dislike. "It tastes odd."

"You get used to it," said Baka tranquilly, and he offered it to some of the others at the table. Several of them sampled it, very gingerly.

"Excellent!" one of them cried. "Where can I get some of this?"

"I make it myself," said Baka. "I can give you some."

"Sell it to me."

"I'm not allowed to sell anything. I am a student at the science laboratories."

"Yes," Aram chimed in. "This is the bright one of our family. He is with the master scientist Lakon."

Everyone now looked at Baka with interest and respect.

"But what is this salt?" one insisted. "I am beginning to like it."

"I make it out of the sea," Baka said.

He had made it of dried and powdered sea creatures that he had caught himself. He had suggested to the master scientist that he wanted to carry out a small experiment on his own and had been allowed to do this. Baka had learned, by reading some very old manuscripts, that in ancient times—very ancient times, almost beyond the memory of man—people had eaten flesh, the flesh of sea creatures, of animals, even of other men. The thought had repelled him only momentarily. As he read descriptions of the excitement brought on by the smell of roasting flesh, he began to wish to taste some himself and he started to wonder why Atlanteans were vegetarians.

He had asked the master scientist, who had been busy thinking of a new procedure for measuring the stored power in his crystal. "Oh, I think it was because the eating of flesh makes men aggressive and warlike," he had answered carelessly. "We are a higher race; we despise war. Life belongs to the Great Spirit: only He can give it; only He can take it away. Those primitive flesh-eaters destroyed themselves far back in the dawn of history; they fought against each other until almost all men on earth were exterminated. Then our own race came here. The Sages say we came from other kingdoms in the clouds and that we came in chariots driven by the sun's power. And we are peaceful. We are thinkers. We do not eat flesh and we do not wage war."

"But," commented Baka, "we seem to have lost some of the arts of our first ancestors, the race the Sages speak of. Perhaps a little aggression would make our minds keener, our interests more fierce and immediate."

"Maybe. I myself would not like to eat flesh. The flesh of a dead creature? How revolting."

And Baka had reasoned that what was denied almost always took on special attractions for many men. Perhaps he could teach some to like flesh and so build up in them a secret vice. This would be the best way to get people to follow him blindly and do his bidding. If he could teach men to crave the forbidden flesh, he could make them his creatures, his slaves.

He began with the dried and powdered flesh of the sea animals. And immediately he saw that several of the men would appreciate it even more if they thought it forbidden.

Pleased with the beginning he had made among Aram's friends and co-workers, Baka started for home. The walk was not to his liking; he was not fond of strenuous exercise, and in order to arrive home in time to do what he wanted to do and also to get back to the laboratory before night, he would have to hurry. Grumpily, he hurried along.

As he came into view of the cove and the saffron fields, he stood and looked and was astounded. It was obvious that there had been great destruction. Had the storm, his storm, done this? Baka began to feel the trembling excitement that always came when he saw the solution of a problem clearly while still involved in mathematical calculations.

He went first to the house to salute his mother. She came running toward him when she saw him, and gave him a swift embrace.

"Do you eat well?" she asked anxiously. "You look so thin. Have you been all right?"

"I was worried about what had happened to you all during the storm. You know I cannot capture or communicate thoughts, as Atlanta does," he added petulantly.

As ever, Mara felt chilled. She always received her youngest child with a rush of love for him and always, after a moment or two, she was disconcerted or angry. I suppose he cannot help it, she thought.

"We suffered. The crops were about half spoiled and there is new construction to be done. But those things can be borne. We lost no one, thank heavens. So, on the whole, we were fortunate. Of course, the cove protected us, and the caves. Some of the people farther up the coast, whose houses face the open sea, lost their homes, and a few were washed away. But come in and have some refreshment." She led him into the hall and made him sit down and slip off his dusty sandals.

"Set is here. He came to visit Aurora," she said shyly, looking at Baka to see how he would take the implications of this news.

"But Aram is in Hesperidia—I just saw him. Oh. Set is courting Aurora?"

"Yes. Your father seems to think him an estimable young man."

"I am sure he is," said Baka, boiling with jealousy.

"Will he be here awhile, or is he going back to Hesperidia tonight?"

"I think he will return on the late tide. He came by boat. You might return with him."

"That would be good," murmured Baka, who did not relish the idea of a long trudge back to the city.

13

S E T had borrowed a small swift boat with a sail, just large enough to accommodate him and one other. He and Baka set sail with the tide, under a bright moon. The sea was not smooth, and Baka felt the swelling and slapping waves with unease, but it was better than walking. And Set was a skillful sailor. Besides, Set was eager to court the favor and approval of every one of the Archers.

"You must have been out at sea when the storm struck," ventured Baka.

"I was. It is a miracle that I am here today." Set spoke the Atlantean language correctly but somewhat slowly, and he had to raise his voice to make himself heard over the humming of the wind in the sail and the dashing of the waves. "I saw it strike. There was a fierce thunderbolt from the sky, streaking purple and silver. Where it struck, we saw a great mushroom of water rise into the air and hover like a bird and then fall. And, all around, the water seemed to boil. And, indeed, it was hot to the touch. A very queer thing; I never saw anything like it before."

"Perhaps it was the vengeance of some god," suggested Baka, rejoicing inwardly. His storm! What a demon the Power Stone could be—and the master scientist had not yet finished filling it with solar force!

"What god?" asked Set reasonably. "That thunderbolt harmed the Great Ocean. Why should the Eternal Spirit wish to harm one of His own? It was—it must have been —some sort of accident."

"Are there such accidents in the cosmos?" asked Baka scornfully.

"Who knows? Only, I am sure this thunderbolt did not come from any of the gods. There was too much evil in it."

Baka stirred restlessly; the flying spray had dampened his clothes, and he was sensitive to cold. "How can you say that? Isn't a storm at sea evil? It does as much harm as a thunderbolt."

"A storm at sea is the Great Ocean in a rage. But I had a feeling—maybe I am learning to capture thoughts, like Atlanta—I had a feeling that there was some human evil in that vicious streak of light."

"You are fanciful," said Baka.

"Perhaps."

They had rounded the point, and the lights of Hesperidia twinkled in a great half circle. Set skillfully brought the boat into harbor and drew it up to the docks. Aram stood on the pier waiting for them. He had a dark woolen cloak in his hands.

"I thought you were coming together and that Baka would be shivering," he said, folding the cloak around his younger brother.

"Thank you," Baka said through trembling lips. He was bitterly resentful that Aram could catch thoughts. Why could he not, himself? It was an unceasing hurt to him and made him press on relentlessly to acquire some other power, an even greater one.

Carefully, he thanked Set and his brother and started up the hill toward the laboratory. As his slight figure disappeared up the moonlit street, Set laid a hand on Aram's arm.

"Aram, you know my interest in Aurora. And I can tell you that I love everyone of your family. I love and respect them. But—" Set looked unhappily up the street along which Baka had gone. "I cannot understand your brother Baka. There is something—something—"

"Perhaps it is his brilliance," offered Aram. "Lakon says that he has the best brain of any student they have had in his memory. I really think they are getting him ready to be a master scientist himself in the future."

Set shook his head. "He inspired a curious feeling in me. Almost like fear."

Aram laughed as he led his friend back toward the dormitory near the docks where he would sleep before tak-

ing his ship out to Egypt again. Meanwhile, he was pur-
chasing cargo and loading.

"Fear? Never. Baka is harmless."

"I am not so sure," murmured Set.

14

AT the temple Atlanta was very busy.
Her days were ordered and she was in constant
attendance at classes, meditations, and labors. The
Priestesses of the Sea carried out many works of charity,
and the novices were endlessly occupied making neck-
laces and coronets of shells, polishing other shells, grinding some of the finest of the pearl shells in mortars with
various fruit juices to make curative creams, and bottling
sea water steeped with special herbs for lotions and as-
tringents.

They performed certain scientific tasks for the master
mariners and seamen, too, making great maps which
showed the whirlpools and counter-tides and shoals
along the coast. There were other maps that gave sound-

ings, showed where there was a great stagnant and still place in the ocean which had grown up to thick weeds and forests of slimy sea plants, and the underwater rocks that lurked in bays and coves. These maps were constantly being revised as sailors brought new facts, and the Priestesses had one large hall where the novices did nothing but identify, correct, and copy the maps.

Atlanta had been working in the map room for several moons when Selene, the Mother Priestess, came to her one day and summoned her by a light touch.

"There is an Egyptian sailor here who says that he knows you and that he has something very important to tell you for the maps."

"It is Set," cried Atlanta with joy. "May I speak to him?"

"Of course. Follow me."

Atlanta saw Set's broad-shouldered shadow against the clear translucent wall of the reception room, and her heart leaped with pleasure. Because she was attuned to Aurora's thought, she knew that all went well with the courtship and she was glad that Set would join her family.

Set bowed, hand on brow, and smiled at her with pleasure, his white teeth shining in the dark face, his eyes sparkling with his special expression of happiness and good humor.

"I have seen your family and all are well," he told her at once. "They send love. But this you know."

"You are welcome, young man," said Selene before

leaving, "but we are very busy women and I must ask you to be as brief as possible."

"It is about the thunderbolt that I came," said Set. "I saw it. The thunderbolt that caused the great storm. I know where it struck the sea, and I saw how it lifted the water. Perhaps you need to know this for your maps. Though possibly it may never happen again. Who knows?"

"Tell me," said Atlanta. "Mother Priestess will know if there have been similar phenomena. What was it like?"

"It was a clear dark night, the sea was heaving and sighing, and we were running before a good wind. Suddenly I saw the whole sky light up with a brilliant flash of metallic light, lavender or silver—I don't know. A thunderbolt."

"But are these so strange? I have seen many such things light up the sky before a storm."

"There was no thunder. There were no clouds. The pressure of the air was as always. There were none of the other things that accompany lightning. And the streak of light was not jagged or flared. It was a long, straight, shining ray of light, like an immense dagger, like a sword, that pierced the sea. And where it struck the sea a great cloud of water rose up very high into the sky and then fell, shining like fire, blazing almost. And the water, even where we were, hissed and boiled and was hot."

Atlanta had grown very pale. "The sign," she murmured. "The sign in the sea."

"What sign?" asked Set curiously. "What do you mean?"

"You are to be one of my family, so my father would wish me to tell you," said Atlanta. And she recounted to him the story of the great angel who had come to their ancestor Drako, and the story of warning which had been told from generation to generation, until almost everyone thought of it as pure fancy and many had forgotten it.

Set remained deep in thought. "But then," he began, "then you must all leave Atlantis. I will take you away, to Egypt."

Atlanta looked at him with tears in her eyes. "Set, that may be necessary. But say nothing. Make no plans for the moment. There may be a way to propitiate the Supreme One. I shall pray for guidance."

15

A K I L and Ramo felt that at last they dared enter the Caves of Light once more, to see what had happened to their work during the great storm.

Vega waited on the shore of the cove, very nervous, for she had begun to love Akil deeply and his safety and happiness were dear to her. She had never been inside the caves and she feared them.

The two young men took their skiff out upon the water and drew in close to the narrow, shallow opening of the Violet Cave. At the moment they thought just right, they bowed their heads low, crouched down in the skiff, and pushed it through the opening.

Akil was almost afraid to open his eyes and look.

"Akil!" cried Ramo, exultant. "Nothing has happened! The cave kept everything safe all through the storm. There are our hooks set into blocks of wood let into the cave walls; there could have swung sleeping hammocks, and not even water would have reached up to touch them!"

Akil stood up in the boat and examined the ceiling and the upper walls of the cave. They were dry, even warm to the touch.

"It is as Atlanta said—a refuge," he murmured. "Well then, we must continue our work, Ramo. Can you go on with it tomorrow between the tides? I shall walk to Hesperidia and tell Atlanta."

"Maybe Aurora could send her the message; they are so close in thought."

"Yes. But now I must get Atlanta's instructions," said Akil humbly. "She knows best what to do. Let us go now. We should take the good news to Mother and Father."

They emerged from the Violet Cave, looked briefly into the other two Caves of Light, and saw that there too, in the Green Cave and the Blue Cave, the storm had done no damage. Then they rowed briskly for shore.

As Akil bounded out onto the sand, Vega clasped him close. He looked into her brown, loving face. "Don't worry about me," he said. "We must practice sending messages to each other. Many married people can do it."

"But we are not yet married."

"Two more full moons and then, when the third one is at the full, we will marry. I must build us a house meanwhile. Down near the mill. Would you like that?"

"Yes," she whispered. She would like any house he built, anywhere, as long as he came home to it every evening. He smiled, for he read that thought. It is beginning, he said to himself. We will be able to communicate, as Atlanta and Aurora do.

Akil walked to Hesperidia in the late afternoon, planning to sleep at Aram's dormitory and eat at his table and then seek Atlanta early the next morning.

He set out briskly, swinging his arms and enjoying the scents of the afternoon, the salty smell of the sea and the sharp fragrance of the little flowers that grew along the dunes, the gentle breath of cypress trees and the breeze laden with the perfume of rose gardens. Before coming to the city of Hesperidia, he passed the lands where countless red and pink roses were grown, to be pressed for their aromatic oil, which was used in flavoring cakes and sweets, in perfumery, and as a medicine, for it was known that the oil of roses would cure many ailments.

He was not certain that he would find Aram, for now he made many voyages, especially to the other islands of Atlantis, but he hoped that he might. He was not worried, though, for he knew the masters who had taught Aram his skills and who had awarded him his trident, and he knew they were hospitable. He wondered vaguely and unhappily if he should go to call on Baka, too. Perhaps he should, he thought uneasily. Baka made him nervous, so he decided to visit the science laboratory first and have that duty behind him.

The laboratory was on an elevation above the city

looking down on all the houses and trade buildings, the temples, and the canals. From that height the city looked circular, because of the great curve of the tide canals and because so many of the buildings were in the form of a circular tower. The green of trees, especially the orange and lemon trees, and the occasional peach and olive trees in home gardens, spotted the gray and golden stone of the buildings with live color.

The climb up toward the laboratory was somewhat steep, and it ended in a long flight of more than one hundred steps. No wonder Baka doesn't come home often, thought Akil. He is a lazy little fellow and surely he hates climbing back up here to the laboratory again.

The laboratory was always strongly locked against intruders. Akil hauled on the pulley that set up a clanging outside and caused a light to flash on in every room of the laboratory. (Baka had told him this.) Akil waited patiently until the face of one of the masters appeared on a screen set into the gate, and Akil heard the master's voice.

"Who are you and what do you want?"

"I am Akil of the Archers. I would like to see my brother Baka."

"I will send him to you."

The image flashed off the screen, and the voice, which had come to Akil augmented from some chamber inside the laboratory, was silent.

After another wait, an opening just large enough to admit one person swung open in the great gate and Baka stood there, small and insignificant in his brown short skirt and sandals.

"Come in," he said to his brother. "I have arranged for you to have permission."

Akil stepped inside, and shivered involuntarily. He had perspired during his walk and had been standing in the sun. Inside the laboratory walls it was almost cold.

Baka saw the shiver and smiled in a superior manner. "We must keep it at this temperature here," he explained, "lower than outside, because of all the experiments. Heat can spoil many of the delicate studies we do."

Akil breathed deeply, drawing up his blood and pumping it through his veins by a sort of bellows technique. In a moment he was warm again.

"How are you, Baka? Mother worries that you are so thin. Don't they feed you well?"

"I am very well. There is excellent food here, better than at home," said Baka defensively. "It is just that I don't sleep well."

"Why not?" Akil was astounded that anyone could not sleep well. He himself fell deep into healing sleep whenever he lay down.

"It is because I have many things on my mind," said Baka. "I am thinking all the time."

"No doubt," replied Akil humbly.

"I worry about some of my plans."

"What plans?"

"Oh, what to do in the future, and so on."

"But I thought you were going to stay on here and become a master scientist yourself."

"Possibly," said Baka mysteriously. "But I have not made up my mind. Tell me, how are things at home? What about the Caves of Light?"

"That's why I walked over," answered Akil. "I must tell Atlanta about them. You have never been inside them, have you, Baka?"

"You took me once when I was little. Not since."

"I'll take you inside any time you want to," offered Akil. "I know just the right moment. I have never made a mistake in this."

"But if you did? If something interfered with the tides —some power—if you could not calculate on past records?"

"Why, I suppose—"

"What if you miscalculated in some way?" Baka seemed very tense waiting for Akil's answer, and into Akil's brain leaped a thought: Do not tell him.

"I can't imagine. One would probably just dive and swim under water."

Baka shivered. "You know I hate the sea," he said then, angrily. "But come, I want to introduce you to the master scientist here. He has been giving me some important tasks, very challenging tasks."

They went up a long, spiral staircase and into a room near the top of the tower. Here, as in Atlanta's dwelling, there were no doors to separate the rooms from the hall. When the occupant of a chamber wished to be alone, he pressed a button which let down a thin screen that was translucent but not transparent and through which the air circulated perfectly. Lakon was seated at his desk, working on columns of figures. He looked up at Baka with a smile. Before Akil's astonished eyes, Baka seemed to grow, to assume authority and even charm. Was this the boy who was always so petulant, so hostile at home?

"Master, I present my older brother, Akil. You have met my eldest brother, Aram, the mariner. Akil is skilled in the arts of the sea, as well. He helps my father on the land with the sacred flower."

Lakon looked at Akil kindly. "Do you want to show your brother the laboratory?" he asked. "The smaller one," he added warningly. The work on the Power Stone was held a secret by everyone in the building.

"If you could spare me, I would like to walk outside with him instead," said Baka.

"Permission granted. Be back here by In-tide three."

Baka bowed and they withdrew.

Once outside the walls of the science towers, Baka said eagerly, "Let's go down to the shore. Over on the far side from Aram's docks."

"If you like. But I thought you disliked the sea."

"I am interested in some sea creatures that get washed ashore now and then."

The late-afternoon light was beginning to fade.

"I think I had better go back down to the shipbuilding docks," demurred Akil. "I want to arrange to sleep there tonight. Aram can find a place for me."

"They hang up hammocks and sway all night," commented Baka scornfully. "Well, if you want to get down there quickly, I'll leave you here." With a wave of his hand Baka started off to the far side of the bay of Hesperidia.

I wonder what he is so interested in, thought Akil. But almost at once he forgot all about Baka.

16

BAKA, for his part, had not forgotten Akil. As he hurried toward the beach where he had often found shellfish, and occasionally a floundering fish washed up in a wave, he pondered on each brother.

Aram would not be easily drawn into Baka's schemes and might even work against him. He might try to discover what constituted the salty powder that several of the student mariners had found so tasty.

Akil? Baka suspected that he was sometimes in contact with Atlanta. Baka was filled with envy. How wonderful to be able to send thoughts, and to capture them, from the very air. That was power, indeed! No, Akil could not be trusted. Nor Atlanta nor Aurora, naturally. Being women, they were unimportant to his schemes, and they were dangerous as well.

Ramo was left. Ramo was stupid, Baka thought. He might do very well. Yes, Ramo might be just the person he was looking for.

Baka came to the small beach where he had taken sea creatures before. There were some children playing on the beach, watched with lazy interest by older sisters or mothers. They paid no attention to the young man in student dress who wandered up and down, picking up shells. Baka waited until darkness fell and the children were herded home, with cluckings and scoldings and kisses. Then he set himself seriously to his search. He found what he was looking for and then washed out a sand pail which one of the children had forgotten—he could rely on one always forgetting his pail and spade—and set it upon three rocks. He took a small glass from inside his tunic and trained it on a few bits of dried seaweed and driftwood he had gathered, until a flame leaped up. When the small fire was hot, he set the pail upon the stones, with several sea creatures in it in sea water, and boiled them. When they were soft, he pounded them to paste with a rock and packed the paste into a shell. This was the stuff he later dried and made into a savory powder, the strange salt that his victims began to crave and were soon willing to purchase from him.

Having done what he had set out to do, Baka hurried back to the science tower. No one questioned his small collection of shells; they served Baka very acceptably as receptacles for the powdered salty flesh he was teaching Atlanteans to eat.

I must begin to kill small hill animals, thought Baka, so that I can dry their flesh, too. Perhaps I could even get some hold over Ramo with that. He loves to eat and enjoys new tastes. I shall try it on him.

The sign that he was wanted in the Power Stone room flashed on the small screen in Baka's cell. He stood up at once, straightened his dress, smoothed down his hair with his hands, and hurried to the master scientist.

17

AKIL enjoyed his evening with the mariners. They were hearty young men fond of sitting about telling tall tales in the evening light while drinking mugs of fruit juices and snow water. Some of them claimed to have seen an enormous sea animal with a hundred arms, each arm covered with suckers that could drink a man's blood in a matter of seconds. These creatures had one great eye in the middle of the head and could turn different colors, as a girl might blush.

Akil thought: They are making these things up.

"Oh, no," said Aram, catching his thought. "There was even a race of men like ourselves, countless moon centuries ago, who had only one great eye, and they were enormous and very strong. Cyclops, they were called.

The old legends say that when another race of flesh-eating primitive men conquered them, the Cyclops entered the sea and began to live there. Perhaps this animal that our companion has seen is one of them."

"Where did you see this creature?" called another of the group.

"It was on a voyage to the west," replied the one who had told about the curious creature, "past the great Sea of Calm, which is full of twining plants that can entrap a ship. We sailed on, farther and farther west, until we came to a green island where palm trees grew everywhere, all leaning to the south. There, on a rock in a sort of bay where we dropped anchor, was the creature. When we approached it, it turned itself pink and yellow and then it unwound all its arms from the rock and slithered into the sea. Many of us saw it."

One of the young mariners was philosophical. "Perhaps one day we will all slide into the sea, also, and become some sort of strange creature, adapted to life in the water."

Aram laughed. "Right now the problem is to adapt to life *on* the water!"

Next morning Akil set out to visit Atlanta. Many moons had gone by since she had been taken into the Sisterhood of the Priestesses of the Sea. She was allowed an occasional visitor, but this would be the first time Akil had been to the temple.

He looked around curiously, after he was allowed to enter and was told to wait in the small stone reception room. There was a table there and two chairs. Akil saw that the walls were decorated with beautiful shells and that some of the jewelry, dishes, and boxes, and other objects the priestesses made from shells were on display. Also, he gradually became aware of changing soft lights that played over the room and over himself, from a source he could not identify. Suddenly Atlanta appeared.

She gave a happy cry, and embraced him. "Oh, Akil, I am so glad to see you!"

The sister and brother drew back and looked avidly at each other. It seemed to Atlanta that Akil had suddenly become a man. Before, he had seemed to be only her brother. She now saw the breadth of his shoulders, his big strong brown hands, the dark shadow of beard on his face, which he kept clean-shaven, after the Egyptian fashion.

He saw that his sister, who had been so soft and young when she entered the Sisterhood of Priestesses, was now taller and more slender, the strong radiant spirit showing through a thinner layer of flesh. Around her, there seemed to tremble a soft outline of pure light, a very pale blue in color.

"Come, you are allowed to be with me in my work-room," said Atlanta, taking him by the hand. "There we can talk at length, while I continue."

She led him through several corridors and up a stair-way and into a round, sunlit room where there were ta-bles, small controlled flames for cooking or heating, and many dishes and molds.

"I make sweets to sell, and I also make many special candles, using the same molds as I use for the candy. I make the candles of wax and some other vegetable matter, and perfume and color them with flowers. Look!" She proudly showed him some of her work.

Akil tried to find the words to formulate the thought he had in mind. "But you could have done this sort of thing at home, Atlanta. What is the advantage of locking yourself up to do it here?"

She looked at him, startled. "Oh, do you suppose this is all I do?" she said. "No, Akil. I have many hours to myself, perfecting some of the things I seemed to know by instinct. Selene, the Mother Priestess, is a wonderful guide in this. I send my thoughts now wherever I will; I receive messages from people. Soon, if I continue to progress, I will receive messages from the gods, and maybe even some day I will be sent a thought from the Great Spirit."

"I have felt that you send thoughts to me," Akil confessed. "Yesterday I was with Baka and I was about to tell him about our caves, when something stopped my tongue. It was you, I think."

"It was I," she said.

Akil saw then that her lovely face was somewhat drawn and pale and that there were dark circles under her eyes.

"Do you eat enough?" he asked, worried.

"Oh, yes. But I am worried. I pray so intensely, so intensely, but evil spirits fight me and make my prayers come to nothing. I pray for Baka."

"For him?"

"I pray that he will stop what he is planning to do. I

pray that he will turn back from the road he has taken."

There was a short silence. The sun was warm on Akil's shoulders and neck; the smell of the hot wax and the perfume from the candles was overpowering. Atlanta had been busy and was about to mold some tapers. She held the woven thread in the center of the candle as she poured the wax with steady skill.

"I came to tell you about the caves," Akil said. "They seemed unchanged by the storm—as if everything had raged around them—but they were untouched. The tides were so high, you remember, but the water did not rise inside the caves. The hooks I had set into the walls for hammocks had not been damaged. The ceilings of the caves were dry and warm; it was as if some invisible wall had sealed them against the sea's fury."

"Then we can count on them," Atlanta said quietly. "You must keep on adding supplies, Akil. Construct a shelf in each cave, too, on which to store boxes of food. And make certain there is a small machine to make sweet water of the salt in each of the three caves. When the time comes—" she looked far away, and very sad— "when the time comes to take refuge in the caves, we should have everything ready to support life for at least two moons."

"But how would we get the people inside? There are only a few moments when the sea will let us in."

"When the time comes," she said again, "it will be arranged. And I will let you know. Now I want you to practice, Akil. And tell Aurora to do so. Every day at sunrise, and again at sunset, look at the sea, at the farthest line, where the water meets the sky, and make your mind open for me. I will come and speak to you. And I will tell you what to do."

Akil looked at the slim young girl pouring her candles, and simply accepted her words. She would know what to do and he would obey.

He stayed a short while longer, telling her news of home, of Mara and Drako and of the saffron fields.

"When you store the food in the caves," she said suddenly, "you must store three saffron bulbs in each cave as well, and you must protect them through everything. On the voyage, especially."

"What voyage?"

"I hadn't meant to tell you about that," she replied. "I will let you know all about that later."

"If you are thinking of voyages, you must think of Set and of Aram."

"Yes, I do. But do not mention this yet to anyone, Akil."

"Very well. I won't."

"Now we can stop, and you will take some refreshment with me."

"I should be starting for home."

"Yes. But first a drink made of apricots and lemons and honey. Not too sweet. You will like it."

They drank from goblets made of some golden metal into which were set incrustations of polished mother-of-pearl. The drink was cool and delicious.

"I'll come with you to the door."

Atlanta walked beside him, the light folds of her pale

green robe floating as she walked. And the pale blue radiance which surrounded her moved with her.

They embraced and Akil went out. As the door closed behind him, Akil felt suddenly bereft, overcome by a feeling that he would never see Atlanta again. But he shook his broad shoulders and laughed at himself. Impossible, he thought. He lengthened his stride and turned his face toward the cove and the Arches.

18

AURORA sat with her mother in the weaving rooms. Many moons had passed since Atlanta had left them to become one of the Sea Priestesses, and many more since Baka had begun his secret experiments.

Mara and Drako had given their consent for Aurora's marriage to Set, but they wished their daughter to remain at home for at least twelve moons more, and Mara had planned a program of education for Aurora so that she would be able to manage her own household. It had been settled that the young couple would live in Egypt at first, so that Aurora could learn from Set's mother and be a daughter to her. Set would bring her to Poseida often to visit.

"I don't want to live so far from you and home, Mother."

Mara looked up smiling as she added some silvery threads to the pale green stuff she was weaving.

"After you marry, home will mean something different," she told her daughter. "I myself came from the other side of Poseida, you know. My home was far to the north."

"Tell me about it," said Aurora, who loved to hear her mother talk of the olden days.

"You know that my parents were sea people. My father was a mariner, and later on, in our town of Helena, he was Keeper of the Tides, for we also had circular canals there which let the sea in and out by means of great gates. My mother knew and loved the sea; she could sail as well as a man, but of course only in small boats in the bay. She was not allowed to take her skiff out upon the ocean."

Mara stopped and smiled at her memories. "But my mother knew all the household arts and taught them to me: how to cook, to make medicines and to care for the sick and injured, how to weave, how to sew, how to make perfumes, oils, and cosmetics, how to preserve and store food and household goods, the essentials of gardening— all the things I am teaching you."

"But how did you and Father meet?"

"We met in Hesperidia, at a great festival." Under Mara's hands, the soft silken stuff she was weaving took on a shimmer like moonlight. Aurora went on steadily weaving cloth of the finest white wool.

"It was the Great Sacrifice Day. You have heard me speak of it. Everyone who could manage to get to Hesperidia to be present had come. There had been a great storm and part of my own island began sliding into the sea—not where we lived, but toward the east. A whole bridge of land, by which people used to travel far toward the northeast, to the land of fogs and dripping trees, fell into the ocean and was gone. We had been warned of it and we were able to get all the people who lived on that tongue of land safely away before it trembled and began its descent. But the Sea Priestesses feared there might be more loss of land to Poseida; they knew the Great Ocean was angry and so they announced one of the Great Sacrifices."

"How—how did they announce this?" asked Aurora in a quavering voice, for at the thought of any trembling in the heart of the earth—she had felt a few—her heart seemed to melt with fear.

"Just as they do now, by sending messages into the minds of selected people, who are always ready to receive them. It seems to me," mused Mara, "that when I was young more people were able to take and send messages. The skill has been dying out, and it is a great shame. My mother was like Atlanta; she was very gifted in this way. She received the message, and my father brought us, all the family, in his own boat. We were two days on the sea, and it was rough and stormy, for the Great Ocean was still angry and raging against the shore."

The weaving continued. Mara stopped her own work to show Aurora how to weave a silvery border into the wool in a pattern of leaves. The work was intricate and Aurora had to concentrate. At length Mara resumed, "As we arrived late, and there were many boats tying up to the landing docks, we did not have a good place from which to watch. It was then that a tall young man who wore a robe stained pale gold with saffron spoke to my father and invited us all into his place. His own family had a pavilion on the hillside from which we could see everything, and there was room for us all. It was your father, of course, and before we had returned home to Helena, he had asked my father for my hand."

"And you were convinced at once that you loved him?" asked Aurora.

"No. I hesitated, for I had thought I would marry a seaman. I was not sure I would want to tie myself to a man whose family had been landsmen, gardeners, always. But Drako convinced me."

The swift hum of looms as they wove sounded alone for a while in the quiet room. Far outside, children were playing and singing as the teacher gave them their lessons while their parents worked in the fields.

"And the holiday?" asked Aurora suddenly. "The Great Sacrifice?"

"You will be sad if I tell you, but it was a time of great rejoicing. Several of the Sea Priestesses had decided to give themselves to the Great Ocean to quiet his wrath, to beg him to cease swallowing the land. There were three of them, I remember, beautiful young women. They went out into the sea singing, dressed as brides in silver dresses, with their hair full of flowers and wearing the finest mother-of-pearl diadems."

"They were not frightened?"

"Oh, no. They wished to do it. They were full of joy."

Aurora felt a chill, despite the golden sunlight on her bare arms as she worked.

"And was the Great Ocean calmed then?"

"Almost at once. The land shook and trembled and we heard roarings from deep inside the earth, but the Great Ocean did not swallow any more."

"I wonder what enrages the spirit of the sea?"

"We do," said Mara sadly. "Somehow evil always escapes its chains where it is kept captive in the bowels of the earth. Its bad breath filters up through the fissures in the rocks and some people breathe it in and begin to plan wickedness."

"If we could fly—if we could free ourselves from the earth—we could escape it," mused Aurora.

"Perhaps. Well, they do tell that, many many centuries past, some of our people knew how to fly in chariots in the sky, and they were golden godlike people, beautiful to look upon, wise and calm. They were the ones who came down from the clouds and taught us how to grow wheat and corn and brought us the banana, which grows all over our land without any seed, each plant sending up its own children to grow beside it. They were our heroes and have become our gods."

"Yes, I remember. You have told us about them. About the one who brought us the Fire and taught people to use it. And the great goddess who brought the seeds of all the foods that grow in the earth—"

"I will tell all the stories again, so that you may remember them to tell your children, of the gods here and in Egypt and in our northern colonies and in the western colonies—but they have different names in different places. Set can tell you the names as they use them in Egypt."

"And which ones of the gods do you love the best, Mother?"

"I love the Sea God, for whom we named our island—Poseidon—who taught us to sail and to know the tides and whose sign, the trident, is tattooed on the shoulders of the mariners. And I love his wife also, who brought us the cattle that live in the fields and eat the flowers and give us milk."

"I love the Sun God, for his warmth and light," said Aurora, "without which nothing can have life. And the Supreme One, the Great One who is over all the others and who rules all the gods and the skies and all the creatures that live."

"We should love all the gods," said Mara. "Each one has his place. And the Supreme One most of all."

They went on with their weaving, and the folds of soft thin cloth came steadily into being. As they worked, one of the women of the families that worked in the fields came and stood in the doorway. She was agitated and trembling.

Mara stopped her loom and said, "Lea, what is it?"

"It is my little one," said the woman, a sturdy, brown-eyed woman with thick curling hair. "I left him with my oldest daughter, but she fell asleep and the little one is gone."

Mara got quickly to her feet. "Oh, we must find him! How long ago did you miss him?"

"Just at the turn of the tide. They were afraid to come and tell me before, but they have been searching. They can't find him," she ended, and she began to cry helplessly.

Mara went to a great golden gong that hung suspended from cords on her veranda, and struck it three times. At once the people in the fields stopped what they were doing and came running toward the house, and the workers from the processing rooms streamed out and hurried to the veranda where Mara stood.

"Lea's littlest one has been lost. Join hands and fan out over the fields, all the men. Women, join hands, and we will search the beaches."

With low worried murmurings, the people did as they were bid and all joined in the search, save Aurora. She stayed by her now quiet loom, weeping bitterly, for she had heard Atlanta's voice. Atlanta had said to her innermost ear, "The child is in the sea, drowned."

Trembling and fearful, Aurora waited for the people to return with the dead child, for she knew they would find him. But Atlanta spoke again: "Get Akil. He must take the little one to the Violet Cave."

Aurora burst out then and ran pelting down the path

to the mill, where she could hear Akil's wheel turning and the great stones grinding.

"Akil, Akil!"

He emerged, his head-cloth and apron, his arms and shoulders, all powdered with flour, for on this day he was grinding wheat.

"A child has been drowned. They will find the little body soon. Atlanta spoke to me. You must take the child to the Violet Cave. I will go with you."

Akil did not question. He threw off his powdery apron and, taking Aurora's hand, raced for the beach where he kept his little skiff. At that moment they heard the wailing of the mother in terrible sorrow. Far off, she stood with her child clasped to her breast. All the other women began to weep also and to wring their hands and to sway back and forth.

Akil ran swiftly along the beach.

"There is just time, for the tide is almost ready," he gasped. "Give me the little one, Lea. I will take him to the Cave of Healing. Quickly!" Lea did not want to surrender the little limp form in her arms.

"Come with us," said Aurora. "Come quickly, to the boat."

Akil helped them in and shoved off, the boat grating against the wet sand. As fast and hard as he could, he rowed. The women on the shore grew smaller as the skiff plowed the waves. The water had begun to rise at the mouth of the Cave of Violet Light when they reached it.

"Down, into the bottom of the boat, quickly," ordered

Akil, and the now silent mother lay down with the child at her side looking as if he were asleep. Aurora crouched, and Akil, with a mighty heave, sent the skiff through the opening. Inside the cave, the light was a deep violet, and all along the walls of the cave and over the ceiling it danced like a live thing. There was only time to send the boat around the cave once and then Akil dived out. Taking the boat by the stern, he waited for the moment when the incoming waves were at their lowest and then sent it through. Aurora felt the lip of the opening brush across her hair like a rough caress.

Looking back, she saw the next swelling wave completely seal the opening. Lea still lay in the bottom of the skiff with her little one. But now the soft pink color was coming back into the child's cheeks. With a groan he turned on his side and retched. Sea water ran out of his open mouth and he coughed and then cried. Lea sat up, clutching him to her.

"But he was cold," she babbled. "The sea had claimed him!"

"The sea took him, but the Healing Light has brought him back to you. It was Atlanta who sent me the message; she told me what to do," cried Aurora.

All the people, men and women, were waiting fearfully at the beach of the cove. Akil rowed toward them, and Aurora stood up in the prow and waved to them and called, "He is alive! He is well! The little one is saved!"

The rejoicing was general, and Drako ordered that there was to be dancing and music and that many gifts were to be taken to the sea—urns of honey and ointments, and flower wreaths, and aromatic leaves. These were strewn on the waves, to propitiate the sea, for the Great Ocean had wanted the small beautiful child, and the people had snatched him back.

The singing and the music continued all night and by morning the tides had turned again and the swells were serene. The water heaved and breathed softly and the surface of the waves was like satin.

Drako sighed with relief and clapped his hands and rang the golden gong again. "The Great Ocean is not angry with us. He has accepted our gifts! Everyone go home and to rest. We will not work today."

But Vega, who had gone to stand beside Akil and had danced with him all the starry night, slipped her hand into his. "Sometimes the Great Ocean holds his wrath, but he may turn it against us later," she whispered. "The Great Ocean may decide to take you instead, Akil. You are so often on the water! I am afraid."

"Don't be afraid. Atlanta is a Sea Priestess, remember. She will intervene for us, as she did for the little drowned one."

His hand was warm and strong and his words were reasonable, but Vega trembled, and after she was at home, lying on her own bed, she thought she heard the sea muttering and growling far from the cove.

19

BAKA had been promoted to be the exclusive helper of the master scientist in the preparation of the Power Stone. After his first clumsy attempt to use the powerful ray emitted by the stone, he was now learning how enormously dangerous the ray could be. His task was to help Lakon prepare tables telling how much of the ray to permit to be emitted and how to focus it. The master scientist believed that the gem, which had been receiving the concentrated solar power and storing it, would explode, causing incalculable damage, if it took in more energy than could be accurately controlled by man. He therefore became most cautious and decided to put one of the prepared Power Stones into a deep, lightless vault that he caused to be constructed in cellars many depths below the laboratories, and he was now beginning to expose a second crystal to the solar energy. However, now he proceeded on a fixed schedule, making the most minute tests as he went along and calculating the effect on his work of weather, air pressure, intensity of light (due to the season of the year), and many other factors. Baka kept the records meticulously and studied them with great concentration. He knew now that he was in direct line to inherit the post of master scientist in time, and when that happened, he would have complete control of the Power Stones that had been prepared. So he acted with circumspection, was careful, quiet, and respectful in all he did, and became dependable, a man of his word.

This realization had brought to an end Baka's scheme of securing a following that would be blindly loyal to him because he could provide forbidden pleasures. Yet he ached to experiment with the beams of the Power Stone and was sometimes ill for a day or two, so intense was his effort at self-control, so nerve-racking his role of assiduous pupil.

He ceased entirely to have any contact with his family and he never asked for time away from the laboratories unless he knew that the master scientist would also be absent. He was terrified lest the master think of some process he wished to try when Baka was not there; he might then initiate some other pupil into the mysteries of the Power Stone. Baka usually sent out word that he was very busy and could not take the time to visit his family. The Archers talked this over and finally decided to leave him undisturbed and to wait for him to make the first gestures indicating he wanted to come close again to the family.

"If he does not, then so be it," said Drako. "The scientists are often like this. They become detached from human affections. I don't know why this should be the case, but I have known it to happen before. Friends whose sons went into science have told me."

Mara grieved. Baka was her youngest son, and she felt his abandonment and often wept because of it. Sometimes she would ask Aurora, "Did I do something wrong when I was bringing up Baka? Should I have cuddled him more, praised him more? Or punished him more swiftly when he got into childish mischief? Oh, Aurora, I don't know. And now he wants nothing to do with us. Your father doesn't mind, but I do."

"Father minds too," said Aurora, "but he is trying to convince himself that it is Baka's brilliance that has alienated him from us. I do not think this, Mother. I think Baka is suffering too, only he doesn't know it. He thinks he is showing strength in not needing our affection; but this only shows that he is weak."

"I don't know. I don't know," mourned Mara. "Should I go ask to see him? Surely he would not refuse to see me, his mother!"

Aurora was silent. She and her mother were in the special room where the perfume was distilled from flowers. Aurora was watching the small apparatus used for distillation, while her mother sorted and opened the flowers. On this day they were making the favorite perfume of Atlantis—oil of roses. In fields far to one side of the saffron fields, Mara tended a large rose garden, her roses selected for the strength and richness of their fragrance. When the flowers were full-blown, and not a day later, she gathered them in the early morning while they were still wet with dew, and then she and Aurora, or some young woman from one of the families that worked with the Archers, distilled the oil and gathered it into beakers. After the fragrance was mixed with the plain refined vegetable fats, the attar was packed into alabaster vases and then sealed. Mara always had four or five urns of golden metal into which she packed her finest ointments. Set customarily bought several of these from her on each voyage and sold them for high prices in Egypt. Mara now intended to prepare at least a dozen such vials of rose oil to be part of Aurora's wedding gifts.

"If you wish to go, I will go with you, Mother. Then, if Baka will not see you, I will be there to comfort you."

"Let us go tomorrow."

The next day Mara packed a basket with all sorts of delicious foods that Baka had liked as a small boy. She also folded into her basket freshly woven and sewn underwear and a warm shirt for sleeping. Baka had always felt the cold.

Aurora and her mother started out very early and walked quickly. Mara was a tall, strong woman, and Aurora, slighter and shorter, had trouble keeping up with her.

The day was not far advanced when they came to Hesperidia. Aurora looked down at the sparkling sea with pleasure and hoped they might have time to visit Atlanta before returning home. Aram was away on a voyage.

Mara was almost running up the hillside toward the round-turreted science laboratories, which shone golden in the sun of the bright morning. A few large woolly clouds hovered about the towers, promising rain for the late afternoon.

When they arrived, Aurora gave the signal, and they were reflected into the entrance screen.

"Who is there?" came the voice from inside.

"I am Mara, of the Archers, mother of Baka, an apprentice scientist. I wish to speak to my son."

"Kindly wait a moment."

After a short time Baka's face was reflected in the screen. He had shaved his head, in imitation of Lakon, and his face was long and thin. They heard his voice.

"I am very busy, Mother."

Mara spoke in agitation. "What has happened to you? You never want to see any of us any more."

"Oh, Mother, you don't understand," he answered irritably. "I am working on important things—important things!" he cried, stressing the word "important."

"Can't you come out to the gate long enough to embrace me?"

"I told you. It's impossible just now."

And the image flashed off. Aurora and her mother were left standing outside the gate, with their basket undelivered.

"Come, Mother. We will go to see Atlanta. The Sea Priestesses will allow her to receive her family."

Aurora had been afraid her mother would start weeping again, but Mara turned to follow her, stony-faced. Just before they reached the towers of the Sea Priestesses, Mara said, in a wondering voice, "It seems unbelievable. But I must accept it. Very well. I do."

And she never mentioned Baka again.

20

ARAM'S journey was toward the west, where there were many miles of uncharted sea. He had been sent on a mission with orders to gather up and bring back samples of the strange sea plants that clustered together in one spot, forming a great heaving island of vegetation. The place was thought to harbor sea serpents and other creatures of the deep. Mariners never ventured within. They were afraid of being caught there forever, for winds did not blow there, nor breezes lift from the sea. There was a strange smell, both salty and stale. Aram was expected to sail all around the great lake of floating weeds and map it, as well as to bring back plants for study.

In preparation for the voyage, Aram had perfected a small wind machine which could be set into motion at the touch of a finger to generate a breeze, should he find himself floating about in still, dead air.

He had with him only two helpers: a boy named Otha, who was an apprentice mariner; and an experienced sailor, an older man, who had once sailed as far as the Lake of Weeds. This man's name was Polo.

Aram loved his boat, which he had built himself, and took the greatest care of it. He had all his distance-measuring instruments tied to a strong cord which he wore around his neck, for he had heard that some mariners lost their astrolabes and compasses at sea and he was determined that this should not happen to him. He also carried as ballast a tall strong limber shaft of metal, in case his mast should go down in a heavy wind, and extra sail.

They sailed for several days in the direction Polo indicated, and then Aram began to note the rivers within the sea, swift-running currents that had nothing to do with the heaving waves that rose and fell.

"Polo," he said as they sat on deck one evening watching the stars, the sails being tied into position to catch the wind, "let us make an experiment."

Aram threw into the water a light piece of white cloth, which floated along beside them as they watched. And then it seemed to be sucked into a force that carried it swiftly away from them and toward the south.

"I have seen such rivers in the sea," answered Polo. "But no one has ever used them. It is not known where they go."

"Let us maneuver ourselves into the current and take down the sail. I'd like to see what happens."

It was a clear soft night.

Polo replied, "You are the captain."

Aram, following the course of the white cloth, which still bobbed and rushed forward, got his boat into the current and furled his sail. The boat did not stop and idle as it usually did with a furled sail. It seemed caught up in motion, a steady movement toward the south.

Aram commented on this, and he and Polo made calculations and wrote down their speed, their general direction, and their position in relation to the stars by which they steered.

Otha, who had been playing with his hand in the water, cried, "The water is much colder now, Captain! Feel it. Yesterday evening the water was almost warm, warm enough to wash in. But now suddenly it is icy."

Aram took up samples of the water and confirmed its temperature. "This river within the sea must come from far north, where mountains of ice float about in the ocean," he mused.

They continued to give themselves to the swiftly running cold current within the sea and followed it for several days.

Then one dawn they realized that the river had slowed and was moving in a circle, a lazy circle, and ahead of them were the green undulating sea meadows of the Lake of Weeds.

Aram felt excited. He thought he might have discov-

ered the reason for the Lake of Weeds; for if the river in
the sea here became a whirlpool, the water in the center
would become almost motionless and thus the sea plants
could find a safe harbor from winds that otherwise would
move and destroy them.

"Polo, we will set up our sail now and I'll start my
wind machine. We must map this whole green vegetable
island."

The task took them many days, for the Lake of Weeds
was extensive. Aram's experiments established that the
sea river indeed circled and circled the place, ever more
slowly, ever more languidly. At last their work was done
and they could set a course for Hesperidia and home.

21

AFTER reporting to his superiors, the master mariners, with full details about the Lake of Weeds, Aram went to call on Atlanta, for the Priestesses of the Sea were entitled to all information about the Great Ocean.

He waited only a short while before Atlanta came swiftly in. She was thinner than before, and her pale blue aura was now visible to everyone.

"I am afraid to touch you," said Aram.

"Don't be," she answered, giving him a warm embrace. "I have been doing much intensive prayer, very much. It has refined me."

Aram gave her all the details of the journey he had made, the size and extent of the Lake of Weeds, the kinds of currents that prevailed there, and all his meticulous notes.

Atlanta took the notes he respectfully offered her. "I am most happy to have these," she told him. "I shall try to visualize this place, for we may need it, Aram. Yes, if ever there is some great calamity here on Atlantis and the sea should rise up in great fury—I pray daily and nightly that this may not occur—but if ever it should in our lifetime, a boat could go into the Lake of Weeds and there be safe, could it not? The waters would rise but the waves would not buffet it. And with your wind machine we could make sail later, when it was safe."

"We would have to have cutting machines to chop our way through the weeds. In some places they extend far down into the deep."

"Think of that. Think of ways to overcome the weeds, so that you can enter and also leave. Perhaps there might be a way of simply parting them. And you must make and have ready many wind machines for many boats."

Aram frowned. "You see something coming—some trouble?"

Atlanta clasped her hands together and shut her eyes. He saw how thin and transparent the flesh was across her bones. Her long, dark lashes lay against lavender circles that made her eyes look haunted.

"Oh yes, I see, I feel something coming. But I don't know when as yet."

"And the other priestesses, do they also see this trouble?"

"Yes. We have constant prayer to avert it. There are

always two of us at prayer, day and night, to the spirit of the Great Ocean, begging mercy."

Aram paled. "You will take my courage from me. You will make me afraid to venture out."

"Oh, no! Something will happen and the Great Ocean will take vengeance, but we will be allowed to save many. I am certain of that."

She took his hand and drew him to one of the small, mother-of-pearl-covered benches to sit beside her. "Do you remember what Father told us, about the angel who appeared to his ancestor, and about the signs?"

"Yes, I remember."

"There was to be a sign in the sea. Well, Set has told us about it, and we all saw and heard the storm it brought. Now we are to look for a sign in the sky. And later—this is the part that affects us most—a special grace is to be sent to one of our family, to be used for good or ill."

"Surely the grace will be sent to you!"

"No," she said sadly. "Not to me. For, you see, I could not possibly use it for ill. Nor could Aurora, nor you, nor Akil, nor Ramo."

Aram was startled. "You mean Baka?"

"It must be so," she answered quietly. "That is why I pray for him also, day and night. That whatever grace is given him, he may use it for good. But, Aram, sometimes I am so frightened!"

"I have tried to see him. But he hides himself," Aram said unhappily.

"Even from our mother," commented Atlanta. "She

went home in sorrow because he would not receive her."

They spoke for a while of other matters, and then Atlanta saw by the shadow clock that she must go.

They said goodbye to each other with great affection, for they had been very close since childhood.

"Keep your mind open and attuned to me," she begged. "I shall send you messages often."

"I will."

When he emerged from the priestesses' towers, Aram took the canalside walk, but he did not stride along with rapid ease and pleasure as he usually did. He walked slowly, thinking hard all the while, and often he stopped to look down at the great curve of blue bay, tipped on this day with many sparkling whitecaps, and at the swift water in the canal, flowing out to sea.

They had been his friends: the canals, the bay, the sea beyond. Would they ever become his enemies, full of anger against him?

Many moons went by. There were warm, sunny months when the whole island-country smelled of roses and lilies, and later months when the wind freshened and the leaves fell. There were months when rain fell steadily and the people went about wearing garments especially treated to repel the water from the sky. Then they moved into the very cold months, when the air seemed to crack with bright, cold sunlight, when sweet water in ponds and little rivulets and small lakes froze into solid ice. Sometimes, far out at sea, they could discern floating mountains of cold, green ice, which had become detached from their northern shore and were dragged by the tides far down into southern waters.

In these winter days there were ice storms when the rain from the skies turned to ice on the branches of trees, changing the branches into glistening boughs refracting the light into myriad colors, and the grass became stiff and coarse with rime. Then Aram was not allowed to take out his boat, for sails and masts became heavy with ice and decks were dangerously slippery.

At home the Archers and all their families kept indoors, or danced around great bonfires to keep warm. Aurora and her mother prepared hot teas for the people working inside the processing rooms and spent much time weaving, for all the people needed warm woolen cloaks.

Ramo was busy caring for the beasts which gave them wool, keeping them warm in sheltered places, taking them food from his stores. He enjoyed this work, for he felt peaceful and happy among the dumb creatures who could speak to him only with their eyes. He loved the sweet smell of the breath of the cattle and the timid trustfulness of the sheep. Even the mischievous and capering little goats amused him. The hares and rabbits allowed him to look after them and fed from his hand, for he had never hurt anything in his life. Mara and Aurora wove some of their softest and most beautiful lengths of material from hares' down, which the little creatures were glad to yield up when the hot months came again.

Akil and Vega were occupied making the final arrangements for their wedding. Their house was built. It con-

sisted of a sleeping room, a receiving hall, and a wide veranda. They would eat with Mara and Drako. But Vega
had to weave the material for her bedcoverings and cur-
tains, summer and winter clothes for them both, and
treated robes to keep off the rain. Also, it was expected
that she take her bridegroom a stock of ointments and
perfumes, teas, and seedlings of many kinds. He provided
the home and also the adornments for his bride: her
crown and bracelets, her girdle of linked metal, and the
jeweled buckles for her sandals. Akil had found and polished moonstones for Vega's crown and had set them in
a design of moon and stars, in beaten silver, which
showed off her dark flowing hair to perfection. He had
gone himself to the hillsides behind Hesperidia, where by
digging one could discover stones that, when cut and polished, shone deep red or dark green or pale shining blue.
He fancied the pale blue stones for Vega, and he had cut
and polished six of these which he set into wide golden
bands. Her girdle he fashioned of silver links set with
mother-of-pearl and moonstones, and the adornment for
her sandals was of the same design.

Aurora was much excited over Akil's wedding, for hers
would follow. Set had already brought her bridal adornments. They lay in boxes fashioned from sweet-smelling
wood on beds of soft cotton fiber. The crown and bracelets for Aurora were of gold, with many insets of turquoise and coral. Instead of a linked girdle, he had
brought a necklace of cascading links which covered her
shoulders, and there were small golden buckles for her
sandals. Vega and Aurora had pondered long over the

stuff for their wedding gowns. Finally Vega had chosen a pale dawn pink, while Aurora would wear a dress of pure white, the material diaphanous, folded into myriad small pleats no wider than the length of an eyelash. As she walked, this would cling to her limbs and seem to flow with movement, and it provided the perfect setting for her golden jewels and her long golden hair.

22

THE moons went by and the time came for Akil and Vega's wedding. Since they were both from the Arches, the ceremony was to be performed there, near their childhood homes. The newly married pair, after the feasting and congratulations, would simply move into their own house and begin to live their lives as man and wife, still part of the community.

Aurora made many lengths of fine cloth as a gift for Vega, and Mara packed special spices, medicines, creams, and ointments into small mother-of-pearl boxes and into crystal bottles for her.

The day of the wedding dawned clear and sunlit, and the people at the Arches all dressed in their best and came to call out the bridegroom and the bride from their homes. As Vega and Akil emerged, they were met with singing, with music played on flutes, hand harps, and cymbals, and they were pelted with flowers. The young men of the community brought Akil to the marrying pavilion, which had been set up in a central place so that everyone could gather round and watch. The girls brought forward the bride. They had tied her hands behind her back with ropes of woven flowers, and they drew her gently forward with other ropes, like a captive.

When the two met at the pavilion, Akil went forward, freed the girl from her bondage of flowers, and took her hands in his. "I would have you for my wife," he said to her in ringing tones that all could hear. "Will you accept me?"

Vega put her hands upon his shoulders, then took his hands and placed them both at her throat. "I would have you for my husband, and I beg all present here to know that we will be faithful to each other."

Akil turned then and walked to the four corners of the pavilion slowly, and at each corner he said, "Please know, good people, that Vega and I would have each other for husband and wife, for all our lives long, and we promise to be faithful to each other and to rear our children in piety and respect. Is there any one who would deny us?"

No one denied, and so it was considered that they were married. The music began once more, there was dancing and embraces and congratulations, and afterward everyone went toward the well-laden tables that Mara and her maids had set forth.

There were games and feasting all day, and just before

sundown Vega and Akil went first to the bride's parents and then to Mara and Drako to kneel before them and ask their blessing. Then, hand in hand, they waded into the quiet waters of the cove to ask the blessing of the Great Ocean. Turning, they walked into the saffron fields, now especially fragrant with the fall of evening, and asked the blessing of the earth, which gives food. When the first stars appeared, they knelt and asked the blessing of the Great Spirit of all, Lord of the heavens and the stars, and then they went away to their own home to begin their life together.

23

BAKA was now the official favorite of Lakon, and he spent much of his time with his teacher, listening, learning, and waiting on him. He had begun to flatter him very softly, carefully watching to make sure it was acceptable, and to his surprise and secret amusement, the master scientist seemed to develop an appetite for it.

Baka had first suggested that only the master should enter the room where the Power Stone was being readied for its formidable tasks of moving among the stars and the great spaces of heaven.

When at length Lakon wearied and needed help, Baka pretended to be worried that any other person should have anything to do with the master's personal development of the Power Stone.

"Oh, no," cried the master scientist, horrified. "We are all in this research together. There is no one who is the head."

Baka made no answer but by his gestures and attitude implied that he could not agree.

The master scientist wavered. It was quite true that he had originated and started the work and also that his was the mind that had carried it forward. The other master scientists were busy with projects that interested them more directly—one with the effect of artificial light and warmth on plants and on infant creatures of all kinds, and another with experiments to find means of prolonging life and vigor. Still another was deep in studies of the cycles of life in all creatures and was working out a chart of the cycles, how they coincide, where they differ, and how the cycles themselves are attendant on certain fixed conditions of weather, place, and available food.

Baka knew these things, for he had made it a practice to listen carefully at all times, even in the students' dining room when everyone was talking at once. He himself said little, but he learned much. Each master scientist had his favorite assistants and pupils, and the system had always worked very well; for the Council of Rulers, who ruled Atlantis, knew that all men are different and that each man works best at what interests him most profoundly. They had never set forth rules obliging the students to study all the sciences, after the first few years of general training, but left the selection of assistants entirely to the masters.

And so Baka made himself indispensable to Lakon,

the oldest of the masters and therefore the authority over them all, as well as the one whose interest had always been in the stars, the sun, the light, and the rays from above, and their powers.

In his early years, Lakon had studied the effects of the various planets upon life on earth, and he had carefully worked out the seasons when the moon pulled not only the tides but the plants pushing up through the earth, the nervous states of excitability of certain creatures, and many other matters. From the influence of the moon, he had gone on to chart the effects of Venus on living creatures, when Venus was in ascendance in the heavens, and so on through all the planets and stars as they rose into the sky during the turning of the year.

Having found that the heavenly bodies, distant as they were, exercised discernible effects upon living creatures, and possibly on non-organic matter as well, he began to turn more and more to the sun, without which no life could prosper. Suddenly one day it had entered his head to try to catch and hold some of that fleeting power which was poured out so lavishly every day. And, after many experiments, he had discovered that this power could be sent into selected crystals and there held trapped, later to be released at will. It was at this point that he had taken Baka into his work.

Lakon had not dreamed of the power the possession and management of this sun-packed crystal might confer upon himself. But Baka had. The master scientist had not thought of it as an instrument of death either. But Baka had.

Baka had tried one hasty experiment of releasing a minute ray of the concentrated power now in the stone and had been momentarily frightened, but also excited. He now determined to use the master scientist's apparatus and skill to pour some solar power into a small stone of his own.

The first thing to do was secure a proper stone. Therefore, although he had not asked for any time away from the laboratories for many moons, he went at length to Lakon and begged for three days off.

"By all means," cried Lakon, who had often thought that Baka was too serious and that he would get brain fever from studying so much, without respite. "But may I know the reason? Is it a young lady?"

Though the master scientist had never married, he retained an interest in romance and enjoyed hearing about the engagements and marriages of his former pupils.

"Yes. My sister Aurora. She is to be married."

"Oh, lovely, lovely." Lakon rubbed his hands together. "We will lock up the room of the Power Stone, and I shall await your return. I would like a little vacation myself."

Baka went the first day swiftly into the hills where crystals were dug out of the earth, taking with him a small spade and a magnifying glass, so that he could study what crystals he found. He knew that the hills were packed with beautiful stones, for all the engaged young men went there to find gems to adorn their brides, and nobody would notice one more young man busily turning the earth and washing the pebbles at one of the many small, flowing streams.

Baka worked carefully and steadily, though he was not accustomed to the physical effort of digging and walking. Streaming with sweat, he labored on until the sun began to drop down toward the west. And still he had not found the stone he wanted. He was searching for a small, perfect red crystal. There were never very many of these, and he had to give up his search at nightfall.

Sitting down on the hillside, disappointed, he considered going back to the laboratory to sleep but decided against it. His scientific training had intensified a natural propensity to finish any task he had started. He made up his mind to remain on the hillside and sleep there, going at his work again early with first light.

But his robe was not heavy, and the nights on the hillside could be cool and damp with dew. He would have to find a cave or a hollow tree. He would be hungry, but he didn't mind that. Baka had never been much interested in food.

By the time the sun went down into the sea, all the other people, mostly young men who had been digging on the mountain, had gone home to supper and to whatever plans they might have made for the evening. Baka began to look about for shelter.

A short distance away from where he had been searching, there was an abandoned quarry which had been much worked in years gone by. Artists and craftsmen had searched in this quarry for a special kind of stone which was exceedingly hard and could therefore cut and mark lines in metal, even in the bright golden metal that was often worked into vases, decorative plaques, and jewelry. Baka went down to the quarry, slipping and sliding along the hillside. As he hoped, there was a small pit with a considerable overhang of stone from above which would serve very well as a temporary refuge.

Baka ate some of the salt paste he had made from sea creatures, finding it acceptable, if not very tasty, and drank some water from a stream. Then he lay down, pillowing his head on his bent arm, and began to watch the day fading from the sky.

Suddenly the light seemed to separate itself out into bars of color—rose, green, violet, and pink—like a rainbow, and yet it was not a slender arch. The wide bands of color glowed and grew deeper and stretched across the entire sky. Baka sat up, wondering what phenomenon of Nature he was witnessing. He had studied the stars and the heavens, of course, but he had never heard of any display of light in great shining bars like this. The bands of color intensified and trembled and seemed to dance, and then they began moving toward each other, and to Baka's dismay, the whole strange spectacle seemed to be rushing toward the hillside. As the lights came nearer and nearer, Baka saw that the colors had begun to form a figure, a gigantic figure of light which vibrated and glowed and seemed to breathe.

The celestial creature became recognizable as a young man with spread wings.

"An angel," whispered Baka, who had never really believed in them before.

Closer it came and closer, shining against the dark curtain of night, and with a sudden effort it seemed to draw itself in upon itself and become small and solid. Soundlessly, the angel landed near Baka and called him. "Baka. You of the Archers!"

Baka rose to his feet and stumbled forward. "I am here," he answered, trembling.

"My name is Merko," said the creature. "Do not be afraid. I bring you no harm."

"I am not afraid," averred Baka stoutly. And, truth to tell, he was not. The angel emanated confidence and good will.

"Baka, I have come to save you."

Baka bristled. "Save me from what?"

"From the evil you are planning."

"I . . . I . . ." Baka tried to protest that he was not thinking of any evil, but the words would not come.

"You have been dreaming of terrorizing the people, controlling them, making them do your will. Do not deny it. I am only a messenger from above, but we know all things—all thoughts, all plans. We know what you have been scheming."

Baka drew a deep breath. "If you know, you must have powerful forces on your side to tell you of the plans of men, plans not spoken of."

"We do have. Our Supreme Spirit has all power on earth and in heaven."

"Then why is he bothering with me?" asked Baka petulantly.

"Oh," the angel said, smiling, "we shall not bother with you, Baka. I have come to save you, as I said—to save you from yourself, from doing the evil you have decided upon."

"And if I promise not to do anything, what then?"

"Then Atlantis will be saved."

Baka laughed. "Why should Atlantis be punished because of me?"

"If you loose this evil you plan, all will be infected, and Atlantis will go down beneath the waves."

Baka felt a shiver of apprehension.

"I am prepared to offer you a special grace, to draw you to our side, to cleanse your heart of ambition and greed."

Baka thought fleetingly that he must be dreaming. "A grace?" he echoed.

"Yes. It was so promised to one of your ancestors many years ago. We have not forgotten."

"What is this grace?"

"I am not allowed to tell you. It is a power which will come to you, but the moment you use it for evil, it will disappear."

Baka shrugged. He was determined not to stand in awe of the angel. The night had come down, and he thought the creature of light would have to fade into the air soon.

"Baka," said the angel sadly, "you do not look squarely at where you are heading."

"I am not afraid of you, a being made of mist," spat out Baka. "I do not believe in you."

The angel made no answer but began to fade before his eyes. Soon there was nothing to be seen but the clouds and stars of heaven.

Baka felt proud of himself for having defied the spirit, the ghost, or whatever it may have been. He lay down to sleep, feeling pleased, but gradually the complacent feeling left him, and he began to shiver with an unnamed dread.

I'm cold, that's all, he said to himself. My imagination has played tricks.

He jumped up and began walking up and down to warm himself. When his blood was circulating well again, he lay down once more, but sleep would not come, and the night seemed endless. He thought of his family. How he had longed to be first in his father's affections! But Drako loved Aram best. Baka knew that Drako tried to hide this, but he knew it all the same, and it had turned him against both father and brother. Aram had been kind but offhand to the small, timid brother and had lost patience with him because Baka could not bear the sea and would not learn to swim. Mara, Aurora, and Atlanta —well, they were just women, after all. They loved him, but Baka wanted to be admired among men. He had not felt content until he had become one of the science students and had gained the interest and affection of the master scientist.

Through the long, miserable night, Baka wondered whether he might have had a chance to gain his father's and Aram's love if he had forced himself to pretend to enjoy the ocean. No, he thought. In that case, they would have wanted me to study to be a mariner, like Aram, and I could not stand a life on the ocean. I simply couldn't stand it. His stomach roiled at the thought.

Akil and Ramo? Akil was as bad as Aram, a man of the water, almost a fish, in and out of the sea all day, and forever busy at his stupid mill. What kind of life was that for a man of brains, grinding cereals to make flour? No, that would not have done for Baka either. Ramo? A worker among the clods of earth, planting and then digging up flowers, year in, year out. Impossible.

No, thought Baka, I had no choice. Now I must play the man and stay on my course. My own family did not understand me and they never will. But I'll show them. I'll go my way and become the ruler of this island. There used to be kings long ago, before the Council of Elders was started. There will be a king again.

There will be a king again! King Baka!

Dawn was coming up with soft rosy light when he came to this resolution, and with the break of day he felt calm and strong and determined once more.

Almost instantly he found just the crystal he had been searching for—blood-red, small, and perfect. Joyfully he tied it in a cloth and fastened the cloth inside his robe so as not to lose it.

Then he set out for home.

24

IT was Aurora's wedding day.

Set had been with the Archers since the previous afternoon. Akil had taken Set and Aurora to the Cave of Violet Light, and they had bathed in that invigorating color.

Mara and her maids had cooked all the dainties for the nuptial table, and the whole house was decorated with wreaths of flowers. The fragrance of the blossoms reached out and seemed to flow in the softly moving air of the bright morning.

Aurora went to take a last walk among the saffron beds and through the processing rooms. She went down past the mill where Akil had ground the flour from wheat for her bridal cakes. She visited the hives where the bees had made many gallons of honey, dark and strong and faintly flavored with the saffron flowers the bees visited.

She bathed once more in the quiet waters of the cove. As she emerged dripping from her swim, she saw Baka coming along the path from the city, and she called to him. "Baka! How wonderful of you to come to my wedding!"

Baka answered gaily, "I felt I couldn't miss this occasion." He came near and embraced her, though he disliked the salt smell in her hair. "My work cleared up a little," he added importantly, "and I thought I could take the time to come."

Baka had decided, after finding his jewel and realizing that he had two more days of leave, to make one more contact with his family, to study his brothers with a scientific mind and decide whether or not they were to be included in the powerful life he intended to forge for himself.

His parents welcomed Baka as if he had not been gone more than a few weeks. This was somewhat disconcerting to Baka, but he thought they acted thus in deference to Set, to whom they did not wish to make any explanations.

Set was resplendent in his wedding attire. He wore a broad golden collar around his bronzed neck and bracelets on each arm above the elbow. His sandals had tassels of turquoise beads, and his mariner's short skirt was cinched around his narrow waist with a broad leather belt studded with gold and coral. The skirt and headband, in the striped black and red of a seaman, were of finely woven silk, worn over a tight undergarment, slightly longer, of fine white wool.

Beside him Aurora looked especially small and slender. Her white robe and jewels shone in the sun, and she walked in a cloud of perfume. Set had brought her vials of nard and cinnamon from Egypt.

Baka's eyes went to the figure of his father, and he saw suddenly that his father was growing old. There was a slight slump to his shoulders; his whole figure seemed to have grown a little smaller, a little less sturdy. His forehead showed that the hair had receded a little, and his head was sprinkled with gray. Baka's heart gave a small leap of affection toward his father; he took a step forward and would have put his hand on his father's shoulder in wistful comradeship. But in that moment Aram came swinging forward, broad and strong and swarthy, his shoulder showing the proud insignia of his calling. As he appeared, Drako stepped forward, a smile of loving welcome on his face. And Baka's hand fell to his side. In that moment his heart hardened, and it never softened toward any of his family again.

He waited for the wedding ceremonies to be finished and then, without staying for the dancing and feasting, he made his goodbyes and started out toward Hesperidia once more. It was just past noon.

The walk, in the heat of the day, tired him and made him irritable. He did not answer the doorman at the science laboratories, who commented, "But I thought you had three days, Baka! And it is only the second day!"

Ignoring him, Baka hurried to his room, stripped and

washed to refresh himself, and put on a fresh robe. After a short nap, he stepped out into the halls and then went toward the deep cellars where work was being done on the power crystals. The rooms were closed and locked. Good, thought Baka. No one will disturb me.

He had a key to the rooms, and he unlocked the door, went in quietly, and quickly and expertly examined the apparatus. Then, for he had decided that he must be bold, he simply substituted his own small perfect crystal for the great Power Stone on which the master scientist was working, and poured into it the focused blazing power of the sun for as long as his calculations had told him the stone would absorb solar power without disintegrating.

Baka had provided a small box of inert material within which to guard his stone, and he covered it, box and all, with layers of silk and of tightly woven canvas dyed black. This went into a secret pocket he had sewed into his robe, where it would not be visible.

Then he unobtrusively went about his usual work. He restored the great Power Stone to its place, set the apparatus in order and in action, and guided the delicate focusing of the sun's rays as he had been taught to do. He was not surprised when the master scientist Lakon suddenly came into the laboratory.

"Why, Baka! I thought you would be at your sister's wedding!"

"I was there. She is married," answered Baka. "But I do not like the feasting, and I came back here. This is more like home to me, anyway. I have been away from the Arches so long, I am so devoted to our work, that my family are like strangers to me now. I only went out of courtesy."

"I see," said the master scientist. "Well, let us get on with our activities then."

"Yes, Master."

It was not yet time to take action, Baka knew. He must try out his own stone first, realize its power, learn how to manipulate it.

He was in no hurry.

25

ATLANTA had been praying with another Sea Priestess in the Great Ocean Chapel. This room was entirely lined with pink mother-of-pearl, and within it the sounds of the sea echoed eternally, for a small apparatus was hidden in the walls which transmitted the roaring, the dashing, the breaking, and the sighing of the waves.

Atlanta had asked to be allowed to pray for her twin all day, to implore blessings on her marriage and the protection of the Great Ocean for her husband, Set. The permission had been given. The other priestess, many years older than Atlanta, knelt beside her and closed her eyes, swaying to the rhythms of the tides, as they were heard in the room.

Atlanta had felt very peaceful and happy in the morning. She had sent loving messages to Aurora and had received them back; Aurora's thoughts were joyful and proud, looking into what she was certain would be a happy future.

Atlanta had allowed her mind to speed across great distances of blue water to Set's country and to enter his home there. She had seen Set's mother, small and beautiful, merry, and kind, very busy with her household, her cookery, her ointments and embroideries. Atlanta had seen that Set's mother visited the sick and took cool melons and figs and pomegranates to the poor. Aurora would enter a good and useful and joyous home.

The morning developed into the wide bright day, and Atlanta felt the waves of love and merrymaking that came from the home of the Archers, and she allowed herself to be drawn into the family feelings of rejoicing.

But then suddenly she felt something cold slide across her mind, like a snake slithering out of a warm meadow onto a footpath and there waiting, coiled and evil.

"Ay!" she cried out.

The other priestess turned to her. "What has upset you, Sister?" she asked kindly.

"A premonition. Help me, Sister."

The other priestess took Atlanta's hands and chafed them and murmured softly to her, as to a hurt child.

"I must continue," whispered Atlanta. "I must see. I must know what it is that threatens."

She clasped her hands and closed her eyes and stiffened her body into a position of intense and concentrated attention. Then the other priestess saw that Atlanta had begun to weep.

At last she relaxed enough to murmur, "Will there be time—time to escape? Oh, Great Ocean, have mercy!"

She would say no more.

26

AURORA and Set lived in a small house in Hesperidia until he had readied his ship and arranged for, purchased, and taken on his cargo. Then, all the auguries being good for a safe voyage, they made their farewells and on a full and swift tide they set sail.

As they were going out on a morning tide, the Archers were there, at the dock in Hesperidia, to see them off. Aram embraced his friend Set and his sister and wished them well. He gave Set special charts which had been prepared in the maritime schools so that he need never be becalmed. He had already provided him with one of his wonderful small wind machines, to keep the sails full and moving in the direction wanted.

Ramo was there, too, with his parents, waving to Set

and Aurora until their ship dipped below the horizon. Akil and Vega had not come, as Vega's mother had become ill and was nervous and feverish if her daughter was not within call.

On the ship, a long and slender one, there were two small castles, as they were called, one to house the crew and one for the captain, where he kept his instruments and charts. Aurora adjusted quietly and easily to the cramped quarters of the captain's castle, to the narrow hard bench which became a bed at night, to the fact that her husband was in the castle infrequently, for he was busy all day and much of each night on the deck. He had to check tides and plot his course by the stars, overseeing the sails, the condition of his men (there were only six in his crew), and constantly re-checking the condition of his cargo and its balance.

The crew were all Egyptians save one, who was an Atlantean like Aurora. He was Set's best aide in mathematical calculations according to the stars and according to the velocity of the wind and of the tides within the sea.

Alone and uncomfortable though she was for much of the time, Aurora felt profoundly happy. She meditated quietly, allowing the look of the sea all around her, and the covering canopy of sky, to fill her mind with intimations of eternity. She enjoyed the salt smell of the air, and the cold tossed spray, and the curious motion of the boat, which suited her and seemed to give her days a special rhythm of their own. To amuse her, Set brought forth games, which he played with her when he was not occupied on deck. Some were played with small packs of

cards, and others with large designs of one sort or another which constituted an imaginary battleground for
"men," or small counters which they used, according to
rules. And he taught her to play another game, called
chess, which had been brought to Egypt by overland
travelers from the Far East. Set told Aurora about the
people of the Far East—delicately boned people, with
pale amber-colored skin and small, slanting eyes, people
of much wisdom and good humor.

"Aram wants to sail to the west," Aurora confided to
her young husband, "and he tells me that there are rich
lands and people with a splendid civilization there who
carve and work the stone and who compose beautiful
poetry."

"I have heard of them. Some tell that they use the
same names for the stars as the people from the east of
us, and the same signs."

"Shall we go there some day? Am I to sail with you
always?"

"No, my love. I will take you on the sea only to trans-
port you to my home and my mother—or to yours for a
visit."

The sea, on the day they spoke, was smooth, deep
blue, heaving softly, sighing against the ship. "The sea is
tranquil today," he said, "but it is changeable. It can be
terrible in its wrath, as Aram has told you, and as you
have seen. No, you must never be in danger, if I can help
it. You are too dear to me."

They were on the water, without seeing any land at all,
through the changes of the moon. As the new moon

lifted into the sky, slim and golden, they came to an island where Set gave orders to slide into the harbor and drop anchor.

Rocking gently on the water, Set and Aurora spent the long evening alone, since he had given his crew permission to go ashore. It was a gentle and happy time for both. The island lifted from a verdant shore onto very tall mountain peaks, around which swirled veils of mist.

"If you like, we will delay here for another day or two. I want to take aboard some fresh water, and perhaps some cargo. The people are primitive but kind. There is a path up the mountain which affords lovely views."

"Oh, let's climb up it, up to the very top!" cried Aurora.

"That would not be easy," he said, smiling at her fondly.

"But we can go up partway."

The next day, after Set had arranged his business in the town and the crew was back on the ship, he and Aurora took a picnic lunch and climbed up to where the mists began. Shivering a little but enjoying the smell of trees and flowers after the many days upon the sea, they spent happy hours. In years to come, Aurora was to remember the days at the island, and the joyous time of her honeymoon on the water, as part of a wonderful dream.

Aurora's welcome in the large city at the mouth of the Nile which was Set's home was warm and loving, and she found that Set had a large and lively family of brothers with their wives and families. Set was the last to marry. Among them all, they left her no time to grow lonely or to long overmuch for her own island home. She loved Set and was determined to be a good wife, but there were many hours when she yearned to hear the sounding sea on the beach of the cove near the Arches and when she dreamed of her mother, of Atlanta, and of the saffron fields.

She kept her mind flexible and skillful at receiving messages from Atlanta, and sometimes from Aram, and she herself regularly looked for a quiet, silent place where she could sit, fold her hands, empty her mind of everything, blot out the smells and sounds of Egypt, and return her spirit to Atlantis. She became increasingly adept, and before the first year of her marriage had passed, she was able to project not only messages but scenes, pictures, sounds, even scents, at will. She knew that she could do this, for Atlanta told her so in messages that came regularly and with stronger visual power.

Aurora sent this message one day when she had been in Egypt for twelve moons: "We are closer in spirit than ever, though we are farther apart in distance and time."

Atlanta's answer came at once: "That is true. It is one of the great balances the Supreme Spirit permits us."

27

B A K A had quietly begun his experiments to test out his own crystal. He quickly learned several things about it. It would burn a line through a stand of wheat in but one flash of light. And it instantly killed any living thing it touched.

This last interested him in a startling way. The first time he used the stone to kill, it was accidental. He had sought out a lonely field on a cold day when few workers were about and no idle strollers. When he took the small box of inert material from his secret pocket and released one short beam from his crystal, he wished to note how far it would reach and whether it would generate heat and other properties. He saw the black, blasted line of burnt wheat where the trapped energy from the crystal had passed. And also he saw that it had felled a little fluffy rabbit, which lay motionless in the path of the ruined wheat. When Baka came near to the creature to touch it, for at first he thought it had been merely stunned, he saw that it was quite dead.

Baka trembled with excitement.

This then was the "death ray" of which legends had been told. Did the master scientist know that his Power Stone would have the capacity to slay a whole city's population? Baka was sure Lakon never intended that the Power Stone be turned against earth but only sent out into space to explore the heavens.

Baka tried a ray from his crystal on a larger creature—a deer. The result was the same. The deer fell instantly to earth, stiff. When Baka drew near, he smelled once more what he had smelled when he touched the rabbit. A strange smell, like the electricity before a storm: scorched, piercing, unpleasant.

The experiment on the deer posed a problem. There must be no questions, no investigation. Baka could not risk any interference until he had perfected all his plans and had made up his mind to strike. So he spent a long and laborious afternoon digging a grave for the two dead animals and covering their bodies well with earth.

Two or three moons later, he went that way once more and was interested to see that where he had buried the two creatures he killed, no grass grew—not even a weed. The life had left the earth. This puzzled and worried him. But as he learned to use his crystal with more skill, the fact that he had power over life and death began to give him enormous satisfaction, more than he had ever dreamed it would.

In Poseida, and in all of Atlantis, death was never inflicted. It was awaited as a command from the Great Spirit which brooked no disobedience. Thus, many old persons who felt their energies and their life force diminishing to the point at which they could no longer feel useful or do the things that interested them often went up into the mountains, there to pray and to await the summons of the Great Spirit. When the Great Spirit called a child or a young person, there was mourning and sadness at the loss; but the Atlanteans, who lived in awe of the great natural laws that controlled all creatures and all life, did not resist the commands of the Great Spirit. Knowing that all lived only by His express permission, they accepted whatever fate He decreed for them.

Now Baka saw that he could defy the Great Spirit by imposing commands himself. At first this frightened him in a curious way. He did not regret anything he had done, not even the lives he had taken; but he was frightened of revenge, of punishment, from the Great Spirit.

But nothing happened.

Every day he examined his hands, his eyes; his hands were as skillful as ever, his eyes as keen. He tested his brain; he could remember all the most complicated formulae, he could solve difficult mathematical problems as swiftly and as accurately as always.

He awaited a sudden, stifling illness. Nothing happened.

He awoke suddenly one night with the solution absolutely clear in his mind. This was the grace he had been promised!

The Great Spirit has allowed me to partake of His power.

Now, I am like a god myself.

Who controls life and death *is* a god.

I, Baka, am a god.

28

AS many moons slipped by, waxing and waning, Baka perfected his abilities, and he began to choose his lieutenants.

He had decided that those who were to be his followers, his court, must possess certain qualities. First, they must be absolutely loyal to him. The way to achieve this, he thought, was to let the candidate he had considered observe Baka's power of death. He must take him out to the fields or the hills and kill something. That would be enough to establish loyalty, for nobody wants to die.

Second, they must be intelligent enough to obey orders but not so intelligent as to develop personal ambitions and set their minds to figuring out ways of wrenching power from Baka. It would not be hard to find these candidates. Ambitious men who are also intelligent, Baka had learned, are not numerous. Ambition often accompanies merely a wish to follow, to be accepted, and so to progress in the esteem of the highest authority.

Third, they must be young. Young people are easily fired up with new ideas. The older the person, the more likely he is to search at once for flaws in reasoning. Baka had observed this to be so common as to be a law of behavior. Only the very young could accept an idea at once, in all its glory, and not question it.

Fourth, they must not have conflicting interests already established. This last was going to be the most difficult quality of all, for it was not always apparent, even after weeks of acquaintance and study.

Baka had leaned this painfully.

There was a young student at the science laboratories who had entered in the last year. He was, Baka thought, a likely candidate for his coterie of followers. Baka cultivated his friendship in subtle ways, using flattery; for this was one of the best ways to break into anyone's mind and find out what was there—whether there were true depths or merely shallows.

The boy, whose name was Kono, responded agreeably to invitations, talked openly and brightly, was very intelligent and accurate in his studies. The master scientist was beginning to take a special interest in Kono which Baka had been quick to perceive.

But one day, by chance, as they drank a glass of honey-sweetened tea together, Kono looked up at the rapidly sailing clouds in the sky and his face revealed an expression Baka had not seen before. "Are you interested in the clouds?" Baka asked idly, sipping his drink but looking keenly at Kono from beneath lowered eyelids.

"Oh, yes! You see, I want to design a ship that can sail in the tides of the sky, as boats do upon the sea. I am sure I can do it. When I know enough. See how the clouds move, so swiftly, as the wind moves over the sea. What I have to learn is how to construct a sky ship that will not fall until it can reach up into the air and catch one of the winds of heaven. Then, of course, there will be problems of how to guide it, how to use the air currents without striking into mountainsides, and so on. Oh, many many problems," concluded the boy happily. "I hope to solve these all some day. One by one!"

Baka decided that Kono would not do. He could not be diverted into coveting the exercise of power. He had too many other interests to absorb him.

But, little by little, Baka found boys in the science laboratories who would do for his scheme. Baka was by then in a position of much freedom and authority, for Lakon had begun to lose his energies. A strange lethargy often overcame him, and more than once Baka found him asleep, in a deep, dreamless seizure, in the Power Stone room.

One day Lakon woke from such a sleep uneasily, shook himself, and looked at Baka with eyes that could not focus. "Baka," he called in a weak voice.

"Yes, Master."

"There may be some evil effect from this stone of ours, some emanation that penetrates even the inert wrappings with which we protect it. We must study this, Baka."

"Yes, Master. But are there any other substances strong and dull enough to protect the power of the stone?"

"We must search."

"Yes, Master."

"I will go to my room now, if you will help me."

Baka realized that he would not have long to wait. At the same time he turned his researches very keenly toward finding substances through which no hint of the terrible power of the stone might seep. In this he had little success, and uneasily he decided that he must simply exercise great care personally and look rather for a follower who could be taught to manipulate the Stone and who would follow instructions blindly, out of loyalty, so that Baka need not expose himself too often to the emanations.

Quite by chance, he found the trusted follower he knew he would need.

He had gone out alone to the hillside to search for another small, perfect crystal, for it seemed to him that it might be a good idea to have several of them charged and ready for use. He had taken with him his own red stone, which in his mind he called "Small Thunderbolt." After digging and searching until he was tired, he seated himself on the grass and waited for a rabbit or a squirrel to appear on which he might exercise his marksmanship.

When a little rabbit ran along, then sat up and looked at him with curious eyes, he slew it with one beam from his crystal. As the animal toppled over and lay quite still, Baka heard a delighted laugh. Looking around, he saw that a boy of about twelve had been watching and now looked at him with eager interest.

The boy was thin and wiry, with thick black hair in a careless, uncombed thatch, small black eyes deeply recessed, and a bulging forehead. The features were blunt, the teeth small and sharp.

"Come here," called Baka.

The boy came readily, looking with curiosity at the small box in Baka's hand. He can't be very bright, decided Baka, or having seen what he did, he would try to hide from me.

Baka dropped the cover over the tiny hole in his box, which hid the power of the "Small Thunderbolt." He had operated the beam by sighting along the box and then lifting the sliding cover with the pressure of his finger, exposing the opening through which the mortal beam flashed.

The child, somewhat misshapen, with legs too small for the rest of his body, and arms overlong, sat down and pointed at the little box. "Let me," he said.

"No. This box is magic, and only I can use it."

The boy did not stare at him or seem annoyed at having been denied. He merely wagged his head in assent.

"What is your name?"

"Don't know."

"What does your family call you?"

"No family. Nobody," answered the child.

"Well, where do you live?"

A grimy hand was waved about vaguely. "Here. In caves. Under the trees. Anywhere."

"What do you eat?"

"Fruit or roots. And rabbits! And birds! I snare them. I like them best."

"Can you remember any other life?"

"What other life?" asked the child curiously.

Baka recalled having heard of lost children, but it was supposed that they lived in little bands, like wild creatures. Sometimes the Council of Elders sent out search parties to find such children and bring them to Hesperidia, where they were washed and fed and cared for, but some of the children hated the city and ran away as often as they could. This must be one of those who did not even live with the pack of wild boys.

"I will give you a name," said Baka. "I will call you Noki."

The boy laughed delightedly.

"And I," said Baka, pointing to himself, "am Baka."

"Noki. Baka." The boy laughed again.

A near idiot, thought Baka. But maybe I can train him.

On that first afternoon, he set himself to gaining Noki's complete confidence. Together they searched for crystals, and when Baka found another which would do for his purpose, the small dirty hand of Noki held it with great reverence, and his lips mumbled words to it. He assumed it already to be powerful and even tried to use it, as Baka had done, on a little snake that writhed across the field. But nothing happened and the snake slid under a rock. Noki turned to Baka with bewilderment, holding out the crystal.

"I must take it home and make it magical," said Baka solemnly.

He returned some days later and found Noki lurking about where they had been, waiting for him. Baka had brought bread and honey, and they shared the lunch. Then Baka used "Small Thunderbolt" to split a rock at a distance of about a hundred paces. He explained first that he would do it, so that Noki would watch, and then sighted along his box and released the beam. The rock fell, with a curious wrenching sound, in two pieces. Noki's eyes rested on Baka a long time, and then he crept close to Baka and nestled to his side, trembling.

"Don't be afraid," said Baka. "If you do everything I tell you, if you are always obedient and good, I will never send 'Small Thunderbolt' after you."

Baka had his first follower, one who would be loyal to the end.

29

NOKI resisted going to live anywhere in the city. Baka was willing to arrange for him to have a room and food somewhere, but the boy preferred the free life in the hills. It shortly became obvious to Baka that Noki was of more value living as he did, like a wild creature, for he brought in other boys—strange half-wild children who were strong and tireless, clever at hiding, remorseless in pursuing whatever ends they decided upon in order to get food. Under Noki's leadership, all became servitors of Baka, who used his "Small Thunderbolt" for them regularly, killing rabbits, squirrels, birds, and even deer for them to eat. Often the wild children ate the meat of these animals raw, but when there were enough of them to defend their fire, they roasted it. Baka sometimes joined them in the feasts, and he began to look forward to them; his mouth watered when he thought of the smell and taste of roasted flesh. At the same time he found that the meat affected him in unexpected ways. He felt stronger, more aggressive, more confident with every day that passed, and it seemed to him that he could see the wild boys too taking on muscle, vigor, and energy.

The Atlanteans had been fools to change, to give up their carnivorous diet centuries ago, thought Baka. True, they became docile and peace-loving, but men should be conquerors—fierce and determined and warlike.

Meanwhile, Lakon was failing daily. He seldom emerged from his room in the science laboratory but left the management of the Power Stone to Baka.

Baka thought occasionally of the angel visitation he had had and of his "special grace." He had worried about the taking of life at first, but no punishment seemed to be forthcoming, and he decided that the apparition had been a product of his imagination. I was tired and over-wrought, he thought, and so I dreamed of the angel and of the threat.

Lakon was now in a semiconscious state and without energy, and Baka persuaded him to sign a document naming his pupil to his post. Since Lakon was the oldest scientist and the authority at the science laboratories, this meant that Baka would succeed to his post, whether any of the other professors was in agreement or not. To protest it, they would have to go to the Council of Elders, but Baka had worked out a move that would take care of any opposition. It was a bold and revolutionary move, but he had concluded that swift blows and suddenly imposed, decisive power were what was needed. He was waiting only for the summer equinox, which was a sacred occasion for the Atlanteans.

The day dawned very fair and clear, and Baka went about his preparations carefully. However, at about the hour of Tide three, two of the scientists and a crowd of students came to him in great excitement.

"Is Lakon well enough to look? Look up into the sky. Something strange is happening."

"Lakon is resting," said Baka. "No one must disturb him now. But what . . . what is it?"

"Come to the top floor, to the observatory. You will see." Baka raced after the others, up the stairs and out onto the top balcony, which had a clear view of the bay, the whole valley, and the wide expanse of sky.

Great bars of colored light were moving slowly across the sky like the spokes of an enormous wheel. Green, violet, rose, golden, and silver they glittered, and everything below took on the color and was momentarily bathed in the strange light.

Then it was not a dream, thought Baka, with a pang of fear. Or is this another angel?

But no angel descended. Instead, the great bars of colored light continued to swing across the sky and over everything below. Then the sun began a strange dance; it suddenly seemed to stop, to tremble, and to move in a small circle. And, as it did so, the earth began to tip and sway with it.

"An earthquake! This presages a great earthquake!"

cried the professors and students, and they ran pell-mell out of the science laboratories, which had begun to sway and creak with horrible grinding noises.

Baka remained transfixed on the roof, watching the cosmic spectacle. Then he rushed below to Lakon's room. There was something he must do first. And afterward, he thought exultantly, I shall proclaim myself. My hour has come!

30

AT the Archers, all the people of the fields and everyone from the processing rooms, all the families, were out in the open, watching the spectacle in the sky.

The earth was swinging and moving softly but not frighteningly. "I hope it will not be severe," murmured Mara. "I pray that the sea will not come up."

Drako studied the sky with wondering eyes. "It is the sign," he said calmly. "There was a sign in the sea. Remember, Set told us about it! Now this is the sign in the sky. According to the prophecy, one of our children will receive a special grace. Do not be afraid. One of our own children, Mara, will save us all. Of course, the prophecy must have meant Atlanta."

Out on the sea, Aram was returning from a voyage to the north of Poseida. He and all his crew saw the great shining wheel in the sky and the dance of the sun. Many of the sailors lay on the deck and moaned in fear.

But Aram was still as a statue. He thought he heard Atlanta's voice, and it was as if she said in his ear, "Sail home swiftly and come to me. We must save many people."

In Egypt, Aurora and Set saw and felt nothing. They were sitting in their garden, eating a late meal of fruits. They had been bathing in the garden pool. Aurora suddenly became motionless, and she lifted her head as if listening intently. Set took her hand lovingly but did not speak to her; he knew that when she became attentive in this way she was receiving a message from Atlanta.

After a short time Aurora's hand became icy cold.

"What is it, darling? What is it?" asked Set, alarmed.

"Set," whispered Aurora, "we must go. There will be a great catastrophe in Atlantis. Atlanta wants us to come. We are to hurry; we are to take people away in your ship."

Set was a businessman who made his living by buying, carrying, and delivering cargoes. He hesitated, much as he loved his wife. It seemed to be a capricious thing to do—to rush toward Atlantis, without cargo, on presumption of trouble.

He considered a mild protest, but Aurora listened again, still as a statue, and then turned to him imploringly. "Listen, Set. Atlanta will speak to you! Listen!"

Aurora leaped up and laid her hands over his eyes, shutting out all light. He heard the breeze in the palm trees and smelled the lilies of his own garden, and his wife's rose-scented hands. Then, miraculously, he heard Atlanta's voice, very clear and precise, in his inward ear. "Please come, Set! We need you. Come to us. The earth has begun to shake and the sea will be angry. Take great precautions, but come."

Set took down his wife's hands, kissed them, and said, "I will get my ship ready. We will go."

31

BAKA called the professors and pupils together by means of the speaker system which connected all the rooms and corridors of the science laboratory.

"Baka speaking," he began without preliminary. "Everyone come to the dining room, please. Lakon is dead."

A startled, silent, and sad group gathered together. There were eight scientists and about twenty-five students. Baka had seized authority; it interested him that no one opposed him as he began to speak. He had taken the precaution of standing on a chair so that he could see every face at a glance.

"Lakon has been ailing for some time, as you know. I believe the emanations from the Power Stone entered his blood and sapped his strength. Just now he died. But before he died, he named me his successor."

There was a dead silence. Baka could see and feel that it was not a friendly silence. There was consternation, bewilderment, resentment. So he went on talking swiftly. "I am to be in authority because I alone know how to manage the Power Stone. The Stone now has so much concentrated power within it that I can control Poseida, Atlantis, the whole world."

He paused. There were murmurs of wonder, some of dissatisfaction.

"I now have full power," said Baka calmly, and instead of raising his voice to deliver this message, he lowered it, almost whispering. "I have full power, full authority. I demand, and I will have, full obedience."

Kono, the boy who wanted to design ships to sail in the currents of the air, stepped forward bravely. "But why should we obey you?" he asked reasonably and waited politely for an answer.

Baka whisked the "Small Thunderbolt" from his pocket and directed a beam at Kono. The boy fell, all life having fled from him on the instant.

"That is why," answered Baka. "Do I make myself clear? I own the great Power Stone and many small ones, and I am now *He who must be obeyed!* Is there anyone else here who objects?"

Silence. The silence of fear.

"Take him up," ordered Baka, "and also the body of Lakon, which is in his room below. They must be buried very deep. I am going to advise the Elders of Hesperidia that I am now King."

He designated two of the strongest students to take Kono away and sent two others to carry Lakon out of the building.

Baka was anxious to make his proclamation on the great voice magnifiers which were equipped to carry proclamations to every part of the city. Also, he was reluctant to look once more on Lakon. The old scientist's face had been pitiful, sad, and disappointed, in that last moment when he knew that it was Baka who was going to slay him with a beam from his stone.

32

THE Sea Priestesses heard the great whirring sound of the enormous speakers from the science laboratories.

As Baka's voice sounded, loud and clear and full of menace, Atlanta's tears rolled down her cheeks.

Selene stood still as stone.

Then she took up the great conch, to sound it and bring all the priestesses from their tasks and into her presence. The conch was only sounded for the most desperate emergency.

"My daughters," she told them in a deep and shaken voice when they had assembled, "the hour of danger has come. We all saw the signs in the sky. Hesperidia is doomed. Atlantis may be destroyed!"

There were moans and cries. Atlanta was sobbing.

"Soon?" quavered one voice.

"Can we do nothing?" wailed another.

Atlanta, still weeping, knelt before Selene and took a fold of her garment. "Let me make the sacrifice! I will give myself to the Great Ocean! I will beg mercy! Gladly I will die for Atlantis! Let me! Please let me!"

Selene dropped a hand on Atlanta's shining head in a gesture of affection. "My child, we have always given up our dearest to the Great Ocean, whenever his wrath was terrible. As it will be, we know. The prophecies have told us. Yes." She sighed deeply. "We will prepare you for sacrifice, my child. All pray now . . . with all your minds and hearts! Pray! Pray for the people!" And Selene sank at once to her knees and began to sway and weep and pray.

33

THE Council of Elders consisted of six men, all over sixty, who had been chosen by the people because of their experience and wisdom. When Baka blared out his pronouncement and named himself King, the Elders quietly met in the home of the oldest to decide what to do.

The oldest of the Council was a tall, thin man, completely bald, but his dark eyes were still lively and piercingly intelligent. He received the others in his garden, where there were many wide-leafed banana trees, roses around a splashing fountain, and two lemon trees covered with fruit.

He motioned the other five to comfortable seats, but he himself remained standing. "I have called a meeting to talk over what we should do," he began. "But of course, we know that we have no choice. We will not be allowed any path other than that marked out by the madman."

"If there were some way we could bargain with this creature," began one of the others.

"We can try. But—"

Another man spoke. "For our own dignity, I suggest that we do nothing—try no blandishments, make no offers, suggest no compromises. But our own dignity is not important. What is important is the lives of the people of Hesperidia and of Poseida."

"The lives of all Atlanteans are in jeopardy," another said. "We must send news at once to the northern islands and to the colonies."

"Quite right," agreed the oldest. "Let us put out our warnings at once."

"And then—"

They were interrupted by a battering at the outer gate.

"They have come for us already," remarked the oldest councilor in a wondering voice. "The matter is out of our hands—"

The gate was opened and a troop of Baka's wild young followers poured in. They herded the old men together like animals and marched them through the streets and up the hill toward the science laboratory. When they arrived there, Baka had them imprisoned in one of the dark cellar rooms.

He could have had them killed at once, but he had decided that he must prepare some sort of trial, so as to give a semblance of legality to his seizure of power. He was confident that he could devise a way of doing this. Baka felt that he could do anything, that he was all-powerful, all-intelligent. He trusted to his intuitions now completely. He felt himself to be a god.

34

IN time Baka chose a splendid house in Hesperidia for his home and administrative offices, while another and more luxurious building was being built for him and his staff. He quickly put all his followers into uniform, so that they should be met at all times with obedience, even obsequiousness. The uniform was black, to distinguish Baka's men from any others, for Atlanteans generally avoided black and thought it a sad and dismal color, signifying the denial of light. Baka's men all wore headbands with one shining stone in the front—a symbol of their allegiance. They were called Sons of Power, and Baka himself began to be called, not King Baka, but The Power.

Life went on for most of the people more or less the

same for a while. Homes were swept, food was cooked, civic and industrial work went on. But, little by little, Baka's men moved in and took charge of everything. They assumed command of the boat-building at the docks; they manned the great gates for admission and release of the tides through the canals; they kept vigil over the fresh-water machines along the sea-water canal.

Soon they occupied the artists' workshops and the factories which made machinery, clothing, and comforts, and they controlled all the food processing and transportation.

Since Baka's men liked hunting and killing, warehouses that sold bloody portions of carcasses sprang up, and many of the people were seduced by the new smells of roasted flesh and by the feelings of strength and power the eating of this flesh gave them.

Baka realized that military discipline and authority were pleasurable to many young people, so he gave them dozens of rules to follow. But, also, he allowed them time off for complete relaxation. In those times they became boisterous, destructive, and excitable, roaming the countryside and the towns, frightening the people and enjoying the fear they inspired.

Young men began to flock to The Power and clamor to join. Those who did not or would not join his black-garbed brigades were persecuted and humiliated by the others. Before many moons, young men who were not in the Power brigades were few. Even the girls began to join into groups, to march and train, and to chant refrains in praise of the Power Stone and the Great Power.

Rumors began going around, in terrified whispers, of the debaucheries of the young Power groups when they were not on duty. It was told how they not only ate flesh but also ate certain seeds and herbs that provided them with euphoric visions and made them think themselves capable of every sort of heroic accomplishment.

It was not long before Baka sent troops to take over the saffron fields.

Drako awaited them when they marched upon his lands. "Tell my son Baka that I will not surrender anything until he comes here himself, in person, to discuss the matter with me," announced Drako.

The leader of the troops, a tall young man who had been a student of chemistry before the Power take-over, had orders to annihilate anyone who opposed him, but he hesitated to take action against the father of The Power. And so the troops marched away.

As soon as they were gone, Drako called in all his workers and spoke to them, for he had received messages from Atlanta. "You see, you know, what has come upon us," he said. "And through my own flesh and blood. Through my son. Now my oldest son, Aram, is coming for us, and also my son-in-law, Set the Egyptian. They will take us away from here. We will go to await them in the Caves of Light, where we will be safe unless Baka unleashes a thunderbolt upon us. All who want to join us, come with us at once. We are going into the caves. All who do not come must cooperate with Baka's people; otherwise, they will be killed. These Power people are ruthless, and life under them will become slavery.

"I cannot understand how we have lost our freedom so swiftly. But it is gone. That is clear.

"Come now, all who are with us. It will take us some time to enter the caves, one by one, but we will start at once."

There was murmuring and there were tears. But the people of the Arches, down to the very last family, came and lined up on the beach of the cove, bringing with them small trinkets and keepsakes—nothing more.

"We have water and food in the caves. Do not bring anything else," cautioned Akil.

He and Ramo worked day and night, taking advantage of the times when the mouths of the caves were free, to pass the people through with their smallest treasures.

Food and water had been laid up long before, and despite the sea below, which surged and sighed softly, the caves were welcoming with a soft warmth. From somewhere there came in air enough so that no one felt oppressed.

When all had been taken inside, when all were resting in their narrow hammocks, Akil and Ramo came in.

"We will be safe, if Aram and Set can get to us in time," said Akil.

"The problem will be the lack of movement, of normal exercise," worried Ramo.

"Atlanta has sent me her thought about that," confided Akil. "I am to go into each cave, one by one, every day, and teach some passive exercises which can be combined with deep thought and prayer. And she has told me that Aram will be here soon."

"I am afraid that wicked man, our brother Baka—"

"Do not call him my brother ever again," said Akil sternly. "He is our enemy."

"I pray that madman will not loose his Power Stone's beams against the sea, against Aram and Set."

"He will be afraid to do it, for the beam would strike too close to Poseida and the turmoil might injure the island. No, Aram will come for us safely, and Set will be in time too. Atlanta has told me that Aram will be here to take away a shipload of people to the west. There are far lands there where they can make a new life."

Ramo was still worried. "But Set? And the other ships he is bringing?"

"Atlanta is taking care of that too. Baka cannot know her thoughts, but she knows his. When he thinks of Set, she will go with all her priestesses to make the sacrifice, and he will forget Set in order to watch."

"He would watch his own sister's sacrifice?"

Akil's lip curled with scorn. "When someone takes the evil road, he soon learns to be cruel and to take pleasure in his cruelty," he reminded Ramo. "That is one of the laws of the Supreme Spirit, so that we can know evil people from good ones. It is the unfailing sign. Baka will be watching Atlanta, and so Set and Aram and their ships will come in and anchor in safety near the cove."

35

P E O P L E from all over Poseida were leaving the island, most of them going north to other parts of Atlantis. Still others managed to get away in small skiffs to start the long journey to other colonies of Atlantis— colonies named for the sons of the great hero-god Posei- don—the islands of Hibernia and of Albion, and the coastal settlements of Iberia and of lands far south of Egypt. Most of these people had lived upon and near the sea all their lives; they loved it and trusted it, and they did not anticipate difficulties other than the hard labor of the voyage and the privations they might have to suffer in new lands.

But there were others who had houses and lands and

who were reluctant to give up all that they themselves and their ancestors had worked for.

"He is only mortal," they said to each other, discussing Baka. "Something will happen to him. We can outlive him, or our children can. Perhaps we can manage to hold on and to stand this regime he is inflicting on us. Let us cooperate, get along with him . . ."

New directions issued every day from Baka's palace. Every day there were new taxes imposed to build up the fortune of the King and the properties of his followers. Every day his Palace Guard and his troops and their officers committed atrocities against the citizens. No one dared to criticize or oppose, on pain of imprisonment and worse. People became afraid to say anything beyond the simplest of comments, for spies were everywhere.

The strangest thing that happened was the manner in which so many young Poseidans were attracted to the spectacle of a supreme dictatorial authority, how so many of them gladly joined the troops for "Control of Peace," and how swiftly they became fanatical imitators of their idol.

"Evil is enthroned," mourned Atlanta in her messages to her sister and to her brothers.

When Set's ship and those that followed him drew near, to within a day's sail from Hesperidia, Atlanta knew the time was growing short and readied herself for the sacrifice. She read, in Baka's mind, that he meant to move against Set and Aram, taking them prisoner and making them bow to his will.

Having prayed deeply all the night through, in the

room where there breathed the sound of the sea, she bathed and dressed in a gossamer gown of blue and green. She wore her jewels made of mother-of-pearl and a crown of flowers in her hair. Her arms were wound in garlands of flowers. She was barefoot.

As she emerged from her room to descend to the waiting boat in the canal, she saw to her astonishment that all the other priestesses were attired as she was—in the ceremonial dress of death.

"But, Mother Selene," began Atlanta, "it is I who offer myself. For you all. To beg mercy of the Sea God."

"We are all going into the sea with you," replied the Mother Priestess. "This house will remain empty. After we are gone, there will be no more prayers. There will be no more Priestesses to serve the mariners and to propitiate the Great Ocean. I have sent messengers into the town to announce our journey out to sea."

Atlanta clasped her hands together and bent her head. "I did not know that I would be accompanied," she murmured. "Then you think that . . . that it is . . . too late—"

"I have seen the vision," Selene murmured sadly. "We have all known of it; we knew the prophecy. The prophetic vision now will come true. This temple, with all it holds, will sink beneath the sea as we shall do."

In silence, the priestesses descended the stairs and stepped into the waiting barge. It had been draped with silk in changeable colors and filled with flowers. Along the canal side, hundreds of people waited to watch them go by. As the barge began its journey, there arose a sound of wailing and lamentation from the older people, and frightened children began to shriek and cry. One of the priestesses beat a deep, slow rhythm on a drum in the barge. The others stood, their heads bowed, their arms crossed.

The moving current of the canal was bearing them toward the water gate, which led out to the bay and beyond to the open sea. Slowly the barge moved forward, as the cries and the weeping of the people surrounded the priestesses in a despairing farewell.

The sound of sorrow and desperation rose and became a loud moan, part of the moaning of the rising wind, which began to tug at the gowns of the priestesses and at the cloaks of the people lined up along the canal side and at the trees and plants in the gardens.

Then, as the barge came to the water gate, everyone became aware that King Baka and his court had taken up positions there. Baka sat upon a throne of shining golden metal, and his brow and arms were circled with bands of the same shining gold. His robe was of rich purple, adorned with the fluffy skins of small animals that had been killed for their fur. His courtiers were dressed in the same manner but in other colors. A band of musicians began to play light dance music as the mourning barge drew near.

Baka turned and gave a languid signal, and the great water gate began to descend along its grooved sides, barring the way to the sea. Baka took up a small mouthpiece which had been made for him and which augmented his voice a hundredfold. "Go back to your house, ridiculous women. I do not want you to make a spectacle of yourselves. I have been patient with you. I forbid you to carry out this plan. If you defy me, you shall feel my anger."

There was a stunned silence from all the people.

Then the wind took up its moan again, and tore at the clothes and the hair of the people, and pulled the draperies of the silken tent under which Baka sat. A clear, high voice rose above the wind's low sound. It pierced the air like a silver wire and vibrated in everyone's ear like a musical string that is plucked by strong fingers.

"Baka!" It was Atlanta. "Open the gate at once!"

Baka stood up, trembling with fury.

"Command the gate to be pulled up at once, so that we may pass through!"

In a shrill, boyish voice, full of rage, Baka answered his sister: "Do it yourself!"

Atlanta's voice called out again, strong, fearless, and calm. "Water Gate, be lifted! So that the water can go back into the sea and let us pass!"

Slowly the great heavy gate began rising again. It rose very slowly, hesitated, and continued rising. The impounded tidal water rushed out to sea once more. Atlanta resumed her position in the barge. Slowly it passed under the gate and out into the bay.

There was a perfect silence until the swells of the bay moved the barge, and caused it to sway on the water. Then Baka's laugh was heard, shrill and scornful. "Let them go! Let the silly things go! They believe in the Sea

God, and the Great Spirit, and in sacrifice and prayer. I could annihilate them all in the time it takes me to open the box that holds the Small Thunderbolt! But what for? They want to destroy themselves. Let them!"

And he gave the signal for the band to play again. Joyful music sounded from the trumpets and stringed wooden instruments and the drums and pipes. But the wind was rising, shrieking like an injured creature, drowning out the sound of the band. On the bay, whitecaps showed and the water was ruffled into angry waves, tipped with a crest of foam.

"Fanatical, senseless women," he muttered. "Let them go."

He strode away, not looking back, and though he was followed by his court, the people of Hesperidia did not leave. They remained, staring out to sea where the barge with the priestesses was bobbing about on the tossing waves. At the very bar of the bay, where the sheltered waters met the wide stretches of ocean, the barge stopped; and the drumbeats, which had sounded through the music, through the moaning of the wind and the splashing waves, suddenly ceased. The wind ceased too, and there was a great sullen silence over the bay and the town. The people at their windows, on the quays, and along the canals were silent, waiting.

One by one, the Sea Priestesses took a step off the barge and walked into the sea, sinking at once. One by one, until all had gone beneath the waves. They had opened a hatch in the barge as well, for it slowly filled with water and then disappeared forever.

Nothing was left upon the sea but a few floating garlands of flowers which drifted on the swells.

There was a great sob from all the people who were watching. "They are gone. All our priestesses are gone."

The sky clouded over with heavy dark clouds, and from deep inside the earth there came a rumble, a growl, as of anger, and the earth began to tip. At first the movement was slow. The world seemed to turn slowly, and then, as the roaring from inside the earth became louder and more terrible, the earth writhed and shook as if in agony, great ravines opened, through which houses and shrieking people fell, and beyond the city, and within it, and in the midst of the bay there shot up flames and molten rock from the furnace at the center of the earth.

Inside his palace, Baka was overcome with astonishment.

So the angel had had the power to carry out its threats. His grace was to be taken from him!

Baka tore out of his palace and ran madly along the heaving and trembling earth toward the laboratory. He would loose the Great Thunderbolt! He would terrify and annihilate the other gods! Sobbing with rage and bitterness, he rushed headlong up the hill, breathing in the sulphurous atmosphere, feeling great pain in his chest, but not pausing even to get his breath. As he came to the gates of the laboratory, there was a terrible rending sound, the earth opened, and slowly, slowly, before Baka's tear-streaked eyes, the laboratory, the dungeons, and the Great Thunderbolt were swallowed by the earth.

Everything—all his plans, all his life—had been taken from him.

Baka lay down on the now hot and shaking ground. He did not even feel when another great split in the earth buried him too, with all his dreams of power.

36

F A R out at sea, loaded with the people of Hesperidia, of the Arches, and of other towns who had
wanted to escape in time, the ships of Set and Aram
rocked on an angry sea. Enormous waves had formed,
rushing in hissing fury toward the shore. The ships rode
the waves far far up, and then swiftly, giddily down into
the low troughs.

When they were at the peak of the tallest wave, Set
looked back, but Poseida was gone. The sea had covered
it.

In his ship, Aram watched with terror as the island disappeared.

Drako and Mara would not look.

Mara mourned for her lost children, for Baka in his

evil, for Atlanta in her youth and goodness. They were both my children, she thought.

She wept for the good people who had gone down with the evil, for all that was gone forever.

"It is as if it had never been—all our life, our civilization, our art, our country," said Drako sadly.

"Gone, and only a few of us will remember it," said Aram. "But we will go on to other lands, to new countries. We will make other lives, and we will always remember our lost Atlantis."

37

A U R O R A shuddered in Set's arms.
Gently, he unwound her arms from around his
neck. "I must go and look after my ship," he told her.
"See to the women and children. We have work to do,
my love. Let us do our work. Life will go on. Life must go
on. There will always be a few of us—a few saved from
destruction and evil who can tell our children about
these things."

Aurora dried her eyes and went swiftly to the aid of the
women who were weeping and the children who were
vomiting and crying from seasickness.

Once more Atlanta spoke into her inward ear.

"Go forward," the faraway voice seemed to say. "Go
forward, as the years go forward. There will be new lands,
new homes. Forward . . ."